SWAMP MONSTER MASSACRE

HUNTER SHEA

SEVERED PRESS
HOBART TASMANIA

SWAMP MONSTER MASSACRE

Copyright © 2017 Hunter Shea
Copyright © 2017 by Severed Press

WWW.SEVEREDPRESS.COM

ISBN: 978-1-925597-57-8

This one's for Norm Hendricks. Dig it.

PART 1
FLIGHT

CHAPTER ONE

Rooster Murphy pried his knuckle out of Cheech's shattered eye socket with a grunt of frustration. Goddamn guy's skull must have been made of honeycombs to break apart like that. Cheech's right eye, in all its smooshed, gelatinous glory, quivered on the knuckle of his middle finger. He flicked his wrist in disgust and watched the eye splatter against the floor, leaving a slick streak.

"I told you to cut it out, didn't I?" he screamed at the Cuban man's cooling corpse. "Did you think I was fucking playing with you? Huh? Jesus, Cheech! You know, you really put me in a tight spot. You really did. You fucked me good, man. You fucked me good."

He hocked a wad of phlegm on Cheech's chest for good measure.

Now what?

All Cheech had to do was hand over the guns, and all *he* had to do was give that entitled Cuban the money. Simple. A friggin' retard could have handled that.

But Cheech, man, he always had to ride him. Always had something to say. Always quick with a joke at his expense. He was Luis Cortez's son after all, so he thought that gave him a free ride to say and do anything he felt like.

And Rooster, he'd really been trying to hold it together. Five court-ordered stints at anger management, meds that made his head fuzzy and his dick soft, meditation CDs made by California fruits, and all that other shit out the window in under a minute.

So now he had the guns *and* the money and Cheech's stiff with the surprisingly fragile skull. It was only a couple of punches. Must have been all that blow Cheech did, eating away at his stupid face.

Fuck it. Either way, he was a dead man. Rough Cheech up a little, you could expect Papa Luis to come down on you so hard you own mother would feel the loss in her old, empty womb.

Rooster took a moment to think about his options. The guy's apartment was straight out of that *Cribs* show, full of all kinds of marble and hi-tech electronic shit. The air conditioning was on full blast and, as he discovered walking into the kitchen, there was plenty of Presidente beer in the fridge. He usually preferred the cheap stuff like Busch or Schaefer, but beggars can't be choosers.

He twisted off the non-twist-off cap of a Presidente and sat back on the big leather couch. Rooster shoved Cheech's legs away with the heel of his sneaker. The cold beer felt like heaven as it sluiced down his chest and into his gut.

This was bad. He'd been down shit creek more than his share of times, but this one took the cake, ate it, crapped it out, clogged the toilet and spilled out onto the floor. Cortez had guys all over Naples. Hell, his arm stretched down to Miami and up north to Jacksonville. Getting out of Florida was going to be like that Clint Eastwood flick, *The Gauntlet*. That *was* pretty badass when Clint fortified a bus to take on an assault from more guns than the French had surrender parties.

For the first time since entering Cheech's apartment, Rooster smiled. He remembered seeing that movie with his dad at the old Big Star Drive-In. He must have been ten at the time. His dad would park a couple of ratty old lawn chairs in front of their Chevelle and they'd eat popcorn one of his succession of 'aunts' had made at home. And on special nights, like the night they saw *The Gauntlet*, his dad would share a few sips of his suds with him.

It wasn't until Rooster had finished the beer that he remembered he wasn't supposed to drink alcohol with his meds. *Do not, under any circumstances, attempt to drive, operate heavy machinery, walk, talk or screw when under the influence of alcohol, because no matter what you are in the middle of doing, you are about to take a world-class face-plant.*

"Crap."

The room spun and he thought he saw Cheech move. The bottle slipped from his hand and his mind slipped from this world.

Frantic pounding at the door woke him up with a start. Half of the beer had spilled onto his crotch, and the amped-up A/C had practically frozen his nuts.

"Yo, Cheech, what you doing in there, man? Quit jerking off and let us in!"

Shit!

Still woozy, Rooster stood and had to wait a moment to steady himself. He looked down, relieved to see Cheech was still dead. Harsh shafts of sunlight stabbed through the horizontal blinds.

"I must have been out for hours," he mumbled.

The fists continued to beat on the door. The tone of the guys outside had turned from playful harassment to growing concern.

"Hey, you okay? We know you're home," a guy with a heavy Spanish accent said.

Rooster carefully crept toward the door. He heard another guy say, "I'm calling his ass."

Cheech's cell phone blasted a Black Eyed Peas tune on the coffee table.

"I told you he's in there. Can't you hear his phone?"

Things were about to get ugly faster than an eagle fucking in midair. As quietly as he could, Rooster ran back to the living room, grabbed the bag of guns, slung it over his shoulder, slipped the smaller duffel bag of money around his wrist and headed for the bedroom.

The door exploded inward with a loud *crack*! Shards of wood peppered the room.

Rooster turned to see three Cuban dudes, each dressed in cream-colored linen pants, tight T-shirts and sandals, come barreling into the apartment.

Was Cortez instituting a dress code?

They spotted Cheech's bloodied body immediately. Rooster didn't stick around to watch them draw their guns.

No sense being subtle now. He slammed the bedroom door shut and clicked the lock. It wouldn't hold them back, but it would buy him time. He went to open the window, but the weight of the gun bag caused his shoulder to drop and his grip on the latch to slip.

Gunshots roared and bullets ate through the door.

Come on, Rooster, man up!

He tried again, this time unlocking the latch and sliding the window open. He punched out the screen and leaped onto the windowsill. It was only a ten-foot drop. No sweat.

The door collapsed under the weight of the three Cubans and they fell, one on top of the other.

Fucking amateurs.

The one on top of the dog pile looked him in the eye as he struggled to get up and swore. "You're a dead man!"

You may be right, Rooster thought, *but not yet.*

He jumped.

CHAPTER TWO

Mick Chella winced as he eyed the sun sitting like a fat, inert Buddha low in the sky. He pulled a bandanna from his back pocket to wipe the sweat from his face, and removed his tattered Red Sox cap to squeegee his balding head.

It wasn't even noon and it felt like the earth was going to catch fire, except the humidity in all its wet, cloying grossness would put it out just as quickly as it started. All the more reason to finish gassing up the airboat and get the show on the road.

"Hey, Chief, how long does the tour last?" asked a juiced-up guido with hair so slicked back from gel that it could withstand a tornado.

"My name's not Chief," Mick said as he screwed on the gas cap. The guido turned to his pal, another muscle-bound, spray-tanned tomato can, as if to say, *Can you believe the stones on this guy? What a douche.*

"I gotta know so I can make sure this piece of tail I got lined up for later knows when to meet me, you know?" the guido said, flexing his pecs under his tight muscle T. His buddy gave him a high five and checked his hair in the glare of his cell phone. Their hair was so stiff, he could have used them for shish-kebab skewers.

It took everything Mick had not to pick up an oar and smash the two of them over the head. Dealing with pricks was part of any job where you worked with the public. Normally, he was fine with it. But on hot-ass days like today, his patience ran thinner than a g-string.

"Two hours," he grunted, walking past them to do a headcount.

Not counting the guidos, there were five others on the morning tour. Seven heads at twenty-five bucks apiece wasn't so bad. The old airboat could seat fifteen, but business in the thick of summer was what it was. Exploring the Everglades in July was not everyone's idea of a good time.

The two blonde girls, identical twins who looked like they were fresh out of college, would give him enough material to jerk himself off to sleep later tonight. In a word, they were stunning. They had all his favorite qualities in a woman: long hair, nice tits (C-cups were perfect: not too big, not too small), long legs, tan skin and crystalline green eyes you could kill a man over. He gave them a wink, but they quickly avoided his gaze, pretending to look at the brochure.

An older couple sat in the two front seats. They were probably the same age as him, around fifty or so, but a better quality of living made them look ten years younger. The guy had the beginnings of a beer gut, but he had all his hair and a well-manicured mustache that must have been dyed to hide the gray. His wife was pretty in a housewife way, with short, brunette hair and a tiny scar just under her left eye. She rested her head on his shoulder and they held each other's hands. Mick had them pegged for empty-nesters looking to rekindle the magic that kids had a habit of stomping into the dirt.

And then there was creepy-loner-guy dressed in a polo shirt and cargo shorts, who spoke to no one and looked mighty fidgety. *Probably hasn't been laid in a decade*, Mick laughed to himself. His sandy hair was parted down the middle with military precision and he had small, furtive eyes. The guy held on to the straps of the messenger bag that was draped over his chest like it contained the cure for cancer. He was strange and nerdy, but at least he was quiet.

The guidos were still on the dock, texting. Mick looped the stern line free and tossed the rope into the airboat.

"You guys want to get on?" he said to them.

"Yeah, yeah," they said in unison, never taking their eyes off their phones. Not surprisingly, they took the two seats next to the blonde twins. The girls gave them a quick look, and Mick was happy to see the lip-curl on one of their faces. Well, well, well, fine as wine and with good taste, too. Maybe he'd ask them if they wanted to see more of Naples after the tour. You never knew. Could be they had a thing for older, rugged guys.

He'd bent down to undo the bow line when he heard two loud pops.

The tourists on the airboat let out a collective gasp. Mick looked up just in time to see a man as large as a mobile brick shithouse running down the rickety dock, headed their way. A big duffel bag flopped against his back and another, smaller one dangled from his right hand.

Mick's time in the service had taught him well what gunfire sounded like. The running man rumbled closer like the dark, outer edge of a killer storm.

There was another *pop* and one of the windows on the Glade Tours office blew into tiny bits.

"Everybody get down!" he yelled, throwing the line and himself onto the boat. If he was lucky, he could get them the hell out of there before those bullets headed their way. It would be close, but it was all he had.

The blonde twins screamed and even the guidos looked like they had crapped their pants.

Mick staggered to the back of the boat and keyed the ignition. The motor roared to life and the blades of the fan began their steady whirl. The boat may have been ratty and made from spare parts, but she still had some fire in her ass. He was about to take his seat when he felt the boat rock to the left.

He turned to see what had caused the boat to dip and barely had time to register the running man's frantic face before a fist that was the size of a Thanksgiving turkey and solid as an anchor smashed into his throat.

Rooster couldn't believe it. A getaway boat, already primed and ready to fly! He felt bad about throat-punching the pilot, but he didn't have time to argue his case with the man.

The guy slumped to the floor of the airboat, and Rooster jumped into the elevated seat and started to pull away. The couple at the front were on their feet and about to make a break for it when he shouted above the din of the fan, "Get back in the boat or you're gonna get killed! Now!"

They looked back at him with pure terror in their eyes. Their attention was then drawn to the Cubans tearing down the dock with guns blazing. He saw bits of the dock explode as bullets buried themselves in an ever closer path of destruction. The couple dropped as low as they could on the boat, and Rooster turned the rudder left and away from the dock and Cheech's minions.

Damn, this boat is big and old. Half of it looked homemade. This was not going to be easy.

Everyone on the boat slid to their right, then backward as Rooster hit it as hard as he could to put some distance between himself and those damn guns. He instinctively ducked when a bullet pinged off the top part of the fan cage.

For just a moment, he considered dipping into the big duffel, grabbing a pistol and turning back so he could give them a taste of their own medicine. But when he bent down to loop his finger through the straps, he lost control of the airboat.

CHAPTER THREE

Rooster cried out, "Godammit!"

The duffel rolled out of his grasp as the airboat went into a sideways skid, kicking up a sharp spray of water that doused everyone on board. He'd accidentally lost control of the rudder, and now they were facing the Cubans on the end of the dock.

He could see their peroxide smiles as they raised their guns and took aim.

This was just the kind of shit they talked about in those anger management classes! He'd let his temper and need to exact payback get the best of him again, and this time he'd delivered his head on a silver platter.

Their guns roared to life, and Rooster felt the air around him ripple with screaming slugs. Because of the noise of the fan, he could feel rather than hear them plug different parts of the boat. The woman in front jumped up from her prone position like a rabbit caught in a snare. Her husband pulled her back down and closer to him.

Shit! Rooster fought for control of the rudder stick, angling the airboat back out to the waterway and his escape. He stepped on the accelerator, and the fan kicked into high gear.

Come on, come on, come on! Rooster willed the damn boat to move faster. Growing up in southern Florida, he'd had plenty of experience operating airboats, but never one this size. It was moving at a turtle's pace, and the rudder stick was fighting him hard.

Using both hands to get the rudder under control and locking his knee so the accelerator was pinned to the floor, Rooster finally got the airboat to straighten and haul ass. It planed over the water and smoothed out nice and proper.

An old-timer in a canoe paddled like a demon to get out of his way, but not fast enough. The airboat clipped the stern with a sharp thud and the canoe spun in a tight half circle, then flipped on its side, pitching the old man, probably out for a day of fishing, into the water. Rooster turned around just in time to see the edge of the canoe clobber the back of the man's neck.

For the second time, Rooster shouted, "Godammit!"

As much as he wanted to turn the airboat around and see if the guy was all right, the thought of giving up even one inch of space between him and the Cubans overrode any sympathy he had. No sense getting everyone killed just to see if some old guy had more fishing days ahead of him. It seemed like a good and proper justification.

The wind felt like a gift from God against his damp clothes. He guided the airboat past other, smaller boats, creating a wake that was sure to capsize a fair share. No longer a floating target, he took a good, long breath, his first since coming to on Cheech's couch.

Safety was false and fleeting. He may have avoided Cheech's gun-toting goons, but when word got back to Cortez, he was a dead man. They had gotten a good look at his mug, and there weren't many folks who matched his description. Cortez would know it was him that killed his good-for-nothing son.

He needed time to think, and someplace where he could do it without ending up with a Colombian necktie. He liked his tongue in his mouth, not dangling out of his severed throat.

Pushing the airboat as fast as it would go, he passed the marker for the Big Cypress State Preserve. The waterways would get tricky from here on in. It would be narrow riding past tiny islands of gumbo-limbo trees and sweet bay. If he didn't slow down, he'd for sure lose the control he'd fought so hard to gain.

Pulling his head out of his own troubled thoughts, he became aware that he still had a bunch of people in his getaway boat. Sensing that the initial danger was over, they had crawled up from the floor and retaken their seats, and now all eyes were on him.

He knew that look. They were waiting for him to make his move, take them out because they could identify him.

Good. That was just the kind of fear he needed. Holding steady on the rudder stick, he successfully yanked the gun duffel onto his lap and dragged the zipper partway open. He casually took one of the guns out, an antique, western draw pistol, and placed it on his lap for all of them to see. It had a mahogany handle and gold engraving along its silver frame and barrel. The damn thing was sweet as hell, and just as deadly. That should keep them in line for a spell.

CHAPTER FOUR

The airboat sailed along the water in bumps and rolls. Over the past two hours, everything had been a complete blur as they headed deeper into the Everglades. A couple of times, Jack Campos thought for sure they were going to tip over as the maniac who had commandeered their tour skated through the narrow waterways. Jack even had to grab hold of one of the young Italian guys, lest he catapult over the side. The kid shot him an angry look, but it was nothing compared to the mug on the angry goliath in the pilot's chair.

All Jack had wanted to do was slip out of the market research conference for a couple of hours and see the Everglades, maybe spot an alligator or two, and be back in time for the lunch break in the hotel's large banquet room. Conferences may be dull, but they weren't deadly.

Jack silently cursed himself and prayed that he would make it out alive.

In the front of the boat, John Almeida kept his wife, Carol, close to his chest with one arm, while using the other to clutch the bar between their seats so he could brace them against the sudden movements of the airboat. Carol wept, but not out of fear. One of the bullets had pierced the metal hull of the boat and torn a crimson gully through her upper arm.

It could have been worse, much worse, but the flesh wound went deep and must have burned like hell.

They jerked left and a wave of muddy water washed over them.

"Jesus Christ, that burns!" Carol squealed. Water and blood ran down her arm, and John had to steady himself. The water was only creating the illusion that she was bleeding to death.

But he did need to wrap up her arm, and soon. There was no way he could do that as long as the thug at the controls pushed the engine as fast as it could go.

He had to get him to stop.

The question was, how?

Liz looked back at the guy who had taken over the boat, then at the pistol, and tried to see if there were any bullets in the chamber. It was an old gun, like the kind cowboys wore on low-slung holsters in westerns. With some of them, you could see the chambers in the barrel if you caught it at just the right angle, and tell if they had a bullet nestled inside or not.

The boat clipped the edge of a sandbar and everyone jounced to the left. The man pulled the gun out of view while he fought to keep control.

Her sister Maddie gripped her arm.

"Where do you think he's taking us?" Maddie said close to her ear. The whirring of the fan sounded like a pride of lions roaring.

"I don't even think *he* knows," Liz said. "He looks kinda confused. It feels like we're just going in circles, but it's hard to tell out here. Everything looks the same."

Liz eyed him from head to toe, looking for any possible weakness. His close-cropped black hair was straight out of Super Cuts. He was about as thick and solid as a pro wrestler, with colorful tattoos of Chinese dragons and koi fish forming two full sleeves. She saw the tension in his jaw as it clenched and unclenched, and took special note of his prison-yard stare. This was a man who made a living out of making regular guys wet themselves with just a look. People like that weren't accustomed to having other people challenge them, especially young girls.

"I saw you staring at the gun. What do you think?"

"Hard to tell. Even if it's not loaded, do you see the size of him? He looks like he could box a bear."

"And probably win," Maddie added.

She was right, but that didn't stop Liz from considering all the different angles they could take. Sooner or later, he would have to stop the boat. She just had to think two steps ahead.

That and stop the Italian kid next to her from copping a feel every time they made a hard turn. For now, he was a distant number two on her list.

Angelo's leg touched the girl's tan, toned thigh, and he couldn't help thinking about how she would repay him for being the hero to get them out of this mess. Both chicks were bangin'. Shit, maybe he could get them both at the same time. Twins. Now there was an incentive to show this asshole what New Yorkers did to people who tried to fuck with them.

Dominic tapped his shoulder and motioned with his head to turn around.

The pistol had fallen out of the hijacker's hand and lay next to the unconscious tour guide's head.

All he had to do was take three steps and he could go all *Mission Impossible* on his ass. Dominic would have his back. He saw the old guy at the front look back. Their eyes met briefly, but it was enough to know that they were both on the same page. The dude's wife was bleeding pretty bad, and Angelo would bet his left nut that he was nice and pissed and ready to stop this ride to nowhere.

They were in the middle of the friggin' swamp. No one was taking shots at them…now. It was just one guy against at least three of them. Maybe the girls and the dork would jump in once things started.

He gave Dom a slight nod, and another to the guy in front.

His internal countdown began. He was going to fuck this guy's shit up good.

CHAPTER FIVE

Nothing was going Rooster's way. So much for making a big show with the pistol. That last near-wipeout had shaken his grip on the gun, and now it was at his feet. Worse yet, he saw that several of his hostages, because that's what the police would be calling them now that word would have spread about the shooting and hijacking of the tour boat, had taken note that the gun was no longer in his possession.

The *Jersey Shore* guys looked like they had steroid-enhanced visions of heroism dancing in their thick heads. He caught their furtive glances at one another and the middle-aged guy in front. Little did they know that the bag had eleven more guns.

There was no way he was about to entertain even the thought of a mutiny. He remembered a safe house, off the beaten path in the Everglades National Park, that his father had shown him a few times when he was old enough to learn the family business. His dad and his partners used the house from time to time to store stolen goods or just hide out until things cooled down on the mainland.

It had been at least ten years since he'd last been there himself. His father and his buddies had all been killed in that shootout outside the Bank of America in Tampa eight years ago.

Eight years in the swamp with no one to watch over its upkeep meant the old safe house was likely in dire shape. Seeing as there were no other options, he had to force himself to remember how to get there. Any thoughts by his hostages of trying to take over the boat and scatter his thoughts had to be put to bed, pronto.

Rooster reached into the bag and slipped his index finger into a trigger guard.

Angelo saw the man take his eyes off them so he could look inside his bag of tricks. Angelo grabbed Dominic by the collar and hollered, "Now!"

They both leaped to the raised pilot's chair, but the rocking of the airboat sent Angelo sprawling over an empty seat and onto his head.

Dominic was faster and slightly nimbler, but his foot got caught under the comatose pilot's meaty arm, dropping him to his knees. His head caromed off the metal edge of the pilot's chair, and he just missed getting his hair sucked into the fan cage.

"Dominic!"

Angelo was back on his feet, and the heavy bag fell off the man's lap. He had another old gun in his hand, but he was having trouble getting a grip. His leg bent and eased off the accelerator. The boat slowed some and vaulted over a small island just big enough to be home to a patch of cattail.

He felt someone stumble into him and saw it was the older guy. The girls were also on their feet, but hanging back.

Time to end this shit.

Angelo and the older dude charged the guy in the pilot's chair. Angelo took him high in the chest while the other guy went low, around his thighs. He felt the air whoosh out of the man's lungs and cocked a fist back to land the haymaker of all haymakers on his cleft chin. Angelo's fist connected with granite and the pain in his hand made his head spin. He looked down to see all four fingers pointing in directions no finger should point in. Each had to have been broken in more than one place.

"My friggin' hand!" he howled in pain.

Jesus, what a clusterfuck! Rooster almost laughed at Jersey Shore's face when he saw his broken hand. Between that and the other kid who'd knocked himself out cold, this was turning into the funniest mutiny of all time. Jack-assery was in full swing with these idiots. Rooster reared back and punched the kid square between the eyes to put him out of his misery. At least the kid wouldn't feel the pain in his hand anymore.

Now he had to deal with the other guy, who had locked his arms around Rooster's thighs and was trying to wrestle him off the chair. As much as he didn't want to, Rooster had to take his hand off the rudder stick and his foot off the accelerator. He brought a knee up into the man's gut and clapped him on the side of his head. The man's grip instantly broke and he fell to the floor, deafened and winded.

"You people are crazy!" Rooster cried. "Are you trying to get us all killed?"

He stared down at the girls, who returned his glare without so much as a flick of an eyelid. The little guy behind them looked away, clutching his man-bag to his puny chest.

Rooster continued, "For crying out loud, sit your asses down before I really get mad!"

He scooped up the gun bag and settled back into the pilot's chair, easing the accelerator down. This time, he had a tight grip on the pistol and aimed it at the girls.

Please just sit down and be good little blondies, he thought.

It took a few seconds, but he had the airboat back in stride and headed for the island of cypress trees that was his first big marker. In this area of the Everglades marsh, there were a ton of little raised islands with cypress trees, but this particular one was special.

The one he was looking for had his all-time favorite number of trees. Thirteen, all nice and bunched up together. His chest heaving from the adrenaline rush that was still coursing through his system, he spied an island and counted trees.

He got as far as eleven when he felt a sharp pain in his ankle and had to jerk his leg back. The Jersey Shore kid who had dinged his coconut had regained his senses and taken a nice bite out of Rooster's lower leg.

"You son of a bitch!"

Maybe a pistol-whipping would keep him down.

He drew his gun hand back and took aim at the kid's temple.

CHAPTER SIX

Understanding that too harsh a blow would kill the moron, Rooster eased the tension in his shoulder a bit and was in the process of delivering a class-A pistol whip when he felt a pinch in the crook of his elbow that sent a shockwave of pain all the way to the base of his skull.

"What the fuck?"

The pistol clattered to the hull and the rudder stick slipped from his other hand.

Christ on a surfboard, that hurt like hell!

One of the blonde girls stood at his side, holding his elbow in some kind of Vulcan death grip. Her thumb was buried in the soft flesh. She gritted her teeth and twisted the pad of her thumb, and another wave of agony rolled over him.

The other chick was now in front of him, leaning against the backs of a couple of empty seats, holding on to their sides so she could keep her balance. She smiled at him, but it wasn't a happy kind of smile. No, sir, this was the kind of smile you gave a cockroach before stomping it to a fine roach paste.

"What the hell is wrong with you people?" he demanded.

Rooster was a big man, and when it came to hand-to-hand combat, he was most assuredly used to being the one in charge of the situation. He was finding it hard to wrap his head around this one. Two fucking girls who looked like they should be home dotting the i's in their diaries with little hearts were handing his ass to him in short order.

The blonde pulled her leg back, then looked at her sister.

"You ready?" she asked her.

The one holding his elbow dug her thumb even deeper and an actual tear sprang to his eyes. Now they were making him cry! This was ridiculous.

"Go for it," she snarled.

The smiling blonde crushed his nuts with the heel of her shoe with all her might.

His breath exploded out of his lungs and wouldn't, no matter how hard he tried, come back. His eyes rolled back in his head and he no longer cared about counting cypress trees or finding a safe place to hole up. All that mattered now was the pain and the fact that he couldn't draw a breath.

Rooster didn't even realize that the shock from the blow to his balls had caused his legs to stretch out and his knees to lock. The accelerator was mushed to the floor and the fan doubled its speed. The boat lurched forward, and the blonde holding his elbow mercifully fell and let go of him.

Going full speed with no one at the rudder, the airboat headed straight for a stand of hardwood hammock trees.

Jack Campos couldn't believe his eyes.

Those two girls were like superheroes! They had taken out that beast in the time it would take to flick a fly off your shirt.

The only drawback was that they were now hurtling full throttle with no one at the wheel. He spun around to see where they were headed, and his stomach dropped so low, he could feel it around his ankles.

Those trees looked pretty damn massive, from the little he could see. The top half of the boat was tilted skyward as they sped, unrestrained, toward land and one hell of a wreck.

Feeling helpless, he reached forward with considerable effort and locked his arms around the waist of the bleeding woman. She was already hurt. If he could do a little something to prevent her from being hurt even worse, he had to give it a try.

"I've got you," he shouted so she could hear him.

Her hand clasped around his own and they braced for the inevitable.

Mick Chella snapped awake in time to see all hell had broken loose.

The running man who had knocked him out was in the pilot's seat and looking like death warmed over. That was good.

What was bad was the fact that he was still giving the gas all he had and the airboat was tilted at a forty-five degree angle, headed God knew where.

Mick's throat was throbbing and his head was pounding, but he had to find a way to get up and get control of the boat. A couple of prone bodies lay around him, shifting with the motion.

Holy shit, the madman was killing them off one by one!

Mick struggled to get to his knees by lifting himself with his hands on the side of the pilot seat.

The two pretty blondes were huddled on the other side and in desperate shape. Their long hair had gotten caught in the fan and it was giving them a free, terrible haircut. He knew the cage would stop them from getting their heads chopped off, but the way it was yanking their heads back looked like it hurt like hell. Their mouths were open wide and they must have been screaming, but he couldn't hear them over the din of the madly spinning fan.

When Mick finally got to his unsteady feet, he looked forward and wished he'd stayed on the hull, blissfully unaware.

Land was coming up fast, and the big trees a few feet from the shoreline were *not* going to cushion the blow.

Mick pulled the guy's leg off the accelerator and the fan immediately began to slow. It wasn't going to stop them from making land like a rocket, but maybe it would prevent them from hurtling into the trees at what felt like Mach one.

The bow dipped down hard, bouncing off the water's surface.

What the?

Mick must have been hallucinating.

On the shore, watching them come straight for it but not even moving a muscle, was a monkey! Or at least it looked like a monkey. What the hell was that doing out in the swamp? And why wasn't it hauling tail out of the way?

The airboat went straight for it like a heat-seeking missile.

All Mick could do was mouth, "Oh sh—"

There was a hard bounce and the steel hull rolled over the poor monkey, then the sound of rending metal as it skipped along the sandy shore, heading straight for the trees.

Mick felt himself floating, and it took him a second to register that he was no longer on the boat, but sailing in the air. The big asshole who had caused this mess was flying beside him. It gave him a warm feeling of satisfaction that didn't last very long, as the trees greeted them both with their unyielding embrace.

CHAPTER SEVEN

Rooster and Mick weren't the only ones to take flight when the boat skidded into the shoreline. Maddie tumbled over the side, her hair freed from the fan, as did Angelo, who was unconscious and unaware, which put him in the best shape of all.

Thanks to Mick's knocking Rooster's leg off the accelerator, and the speed bump that the monkey provided, the airboat slowed considerably. It smashed into a big hardwood tree, but not hard enough to turn everyone inside the boat to Thousand Island dressing.

To his credit, Jack Campos managed to keep hold of Carol Almeida, preventing her from taking a header into the tree. The impact sent him face forward into the back of her seat and knocked out two of his front teeth.

Dominic, John and Liz spilled along the hull of the boat, catching varying body parts on every hard object they could find along the way. They ended in a heap toward the bow.

The fan died, and all was quiet. Turgid water lapped at the shore, but even the buzzing of the insects had ceased for the moment. A hush fell over the swamp as it waited for the first sign of life to make itself known.

Maybe it was a life of hard knocks, literally, that helped Rooster regain consciousness first. He was sitting upright against a tree, and his back felt like it was on fire. He lifted his hand and gently touched the back of his head, wincing when he found a lump the size of Dolly Parton's right tit.

"Sweet baby Jesus, that hurts," he moaned.

The scene before him made him forget his head. The airboat was wedged between a pair of thick-trunked trees. It was demolished beyond use or repair. Several bodies lay scattered along the shore.

Worse still, his small duffel bag must have split open, because crisp twenty-dollar bills lay everywhere. The only saving grace was that there wasn't even the hint of a breeze, so they weren't going anywhere.

He pushed himself to his feet, using the tree as a brace. The world spun for a few seconds, and he had to close his eyes to keep from passing out.

"Come on, Rooster, get your shit together. Just put one foot in front of the other."

He had to get that money. No sense wasting it. He'd be needing it soon enough, once he figured out how to get either to the safe house or out of the swamp. Now that he was no longer speeding along in the boat with the spray from the water and the breeze to cool him down, the oppressive heat had descended like an unwelcome houseguest. Breathing was difficult, and that was not taking into account the fact that his entire torso felt like it had been kicked by a mule.

Walking on unsteady legs, he made it to the wreck of the boat. A few more bodies inside, none of them moving. He felt bad. He hadn't wanted it to come to this. All he wanted was to get away from the Cubans. He'd planned to give the passengers the boat back once he found where he needed to go. Odds were they'd never have been able to trace their way back to him. They were so far off the beaten path, it would be a miracle if they found the dock in Naples. But at least they would have been alive to try.

And he had to admit, he was impressed by the girls. They were some tough broads. It took a lot to impress him. More than just a set of boobs and a nice smile. Nah, they were the goods. Too bad they had to bite it this way.

Rummaging around the stern, he found a bag full of tools, rope and other crap that collected on boats. He dumped everything onto the sand and set out to gather his money. It had taken him a long time to get all that cash, and murdering Cheech to retain it, and he sure as hell wasn't going to let it go now.

Bills were everywhere. A lot of them were caught in a large swath of sawgrass. The sawgrass had sharp edges to it, and his hands and arms got cut up pretty good.

He had to be careful because gators liked to nest in sawgrass. Their tough hides didn't care a whit about the razor-sharp weeds. The last thing he needed was to stumble upon a hungry gator.

Speaking of gators, where were the guns?

Rooster went back to the boat and checked around. He found one of the pistols and jammed it in his waistband. But the bag was nowhere to be seen.

"Nothing's ever easy," he lamented.

The mosquitoes were out in force now and doing their best to suck him dry. He swatted at the back of his neck and face constantly as he wandered around, picking up stray twenties and searching for the bag of guns.

He finally found it under one of the Jersey Shore guys. The dumb dago had landed on the bag. He was facedown in the sand. His Gucci shades were still stuck in the spikes of his hair, but cracked in half. Rooster found the strap by his neck and tugged. The bag came out and the kid rolled over.

To Rooster's surprise, Jersey Shore's chest rose. He was alive!

Now that was going to be a problem. When Rooster thought Jersey Shore was dead, he'd had no problem leaving his body out here for the gators and panthers. When they were done, the birds and bugs would take care of the rest. The circle of life. Nothing wrong with that.

The fact that the kid was alive was throwing a fat monkey wrench in his plans. How was Rooster supposed to navigate the swamp *and* drag him along?

"I'll burn that bridge when I get to it," he said. For now, he had to load up one of the pistols in case he needed to make a point with the local wildlife to leave him be. He found the box of bullets in the bag and slipped six inside the pistol.

Man, they were some sweet guns. They wouldn't take down a charging gator, but they may give one enough incentive to find something else to eat.

Feeling more prepared, he was turning to decide what to do with the kid when the sounds of moaning filled the heavy air.

Rooster looked around, brought the gun up and hissed, "Crap balls!"

CHAPTER EIGHT

All around him, bodies began to move. Groans of pain and confusion were everywhere, even coming from places he couldn't see. It was like one of those zombie flicks where the dead all rise from their graves at the same time.

Only this was worse. These weren't zombies, and he didn't want to go around shooting them in the head. Unless, of course, they tried to attack him again. Shit, he wasn't sure he could do that to the girls *even if* they handed his ass to him again.

He found a stone in the sand and sat down, waiting to see what the final living count would be.

Liz woke up feeling like a spear had lanced her skull in two. The rest of her body didn't feel much better. Her head rested on the Italian guy's thigh. She heard him grumble, and from the sound of it, he wasn't in much better shape.

Maddie!

Despite the pain, she sat up quickly and looked for her sister.

"Maddie, where are you?"

She looked over the side of the boat and found her sister on all fours, marshaling her strength to get up.

"I'm fine, Liz," she said. "Just taking inventory."

Relief almost swept Liz off her feet. She carefully straddled the edge of the boat and dropped down onto the sand. Maddie rushed over to her and they hugged.

"I thought for a moment I lost you," Liz said, holding back tears.

"I'm not that easy to kill," Maddie replied with a pained laugh.

"Uuungh." The middle-aged guy who had landed alongside Maddie struggled to open his eyes. They knelt down to help him.

"What happened?" he said, grimacing when he attempted to roll to his side.

"We crashed," Liz said. "My sister and I took that guy out, but we didn't count on losing total control of the boat."

"My wife, is she okay?"

Liz looked at the boat. "I…I don't know. I saw her in the boat. You want me to check for you?"

He nodded, too dazed to do it himself. Maddie kept by his side while Liz went back to the boat. The woman was coming to, along with the nerdy guy who was fingering the space in his mouth where some missing teeth used to be. The Italian kid was on his knees and massaging his jaw.

"Hey, is everyone all right?"

Her head jerked in the direction of the voice. The pilot—she thought he'd said his name was Mick or Mike—limped toward them. His face was covered in blood that was still seeping from an unseen wound under his cap.

"We're alive, but far from all right," she answered. "Do you have a first aid kit?"

"It's in a metal box by the stern. I'll come up and get it. Think I might need a few things out of it myself." He wiped a palmful of blood off his forehead and out of his eyes.

For the first time, Liz took note of the heat and mosquitoes. It was exactly the way she imagined hell would feel. The buzzing swarm was a roiling, black mass that had descended on everything and everyone.

The nerdy guy scratched a fingernail into the cloth of a seat-back. She watched with revulsion as he extracted a pair of bloody, cracked teeth. He put them in his pocket, turned to her and smiled.

"You never know. If I get back to the hotel, I'll put these under my pillow and maybe the tooth fairy will give me a dollar." He tried to laugh, but it came out as a racking cough, causing him to spit up a quivering gob of blood.

"My head!" someone else was shouting. "I think my head is broken! *Madonna mia*, I think I'm gonna puke."

Liz saw the other Italian guy, this one on the sand about fifteen feet from the boat, rock from side to side on his back, holding the sides of his head with his hands like it was going to come apart.

That's when she saw the big guy, the one who had gotten them into this, sitting on a rock, watching them.

He said to the Italian guy, "Well, at least that'll take your mind off your hand."

The guy stopped, looked at his hand that was more broken up than trailer park after a twister, and wailed loud enough to be heard in the Bronx.

An osprey swept out of the sun-blistered sky and dove into the water, snatching a fish from its merry way, and disappeared over the tree line. Rooster watched it with a burning envy. He'd arm-wrestle the Devil to have himself a pair of wings. Slogging through the swamp in this heat, and later in the dark, could get him killed.

Getting up off his ass was no easy feat, but he made a point not to show the least bit of discomfort. It felt like every bone and organ in his body had been taken out, put through a cement mixer filled with bricks, and shoved back inside, all broken and bruised.

This was some motley crew he had to contend with. He sighed with resignation. The way he looked at it, they were all in this together. It was, when he thought about it, his fault that they were stuck here, some of them most likely gator bait. It wasn't their fault he killed Cheech. And it wasn't like they had asked to get shot at and spilled all over the place in a wreck. In his book, that made them his responsibility. Not that he knew what the hell to do with them, but it would come to him. Getting out of tight jams was his specialty, though this one was tighter than usual.

He'd try to do right by them…unless they pissed him off. In that case, all bets were off.

When he saw that he had their full attention, all eyes shifting to the loaded pistol in his hand, he said, "Let's get one thing straight. I am *not* the bad guy. I was *running* from the bad guys. You just happened to be in the wrong place at the wrong time."

"If you're not the bad guy, how come you're holding a gun on us?" one of the blonde girls said without a lick of fear. She was wrapping gauze around the pilot's head. It bled like a waterfall, but head wounds did that. She may have been young and slight, but she and her sister were probably the toughest in the bunch. Despite the pain and their unfortunate circumstance, it kind of turned him on.

Rooster slowly slipped the gun through his belt on his right side. He moved his hand away and raised both to show he had no intention of using it on them.

"Is that better?" he asked.

She didn't reply.

The ones who weren't dazed shot daggers his way. He had to take control of the situation before somebody did something stupid. When people did stupid things around him, it was usually the last thing they did. The swamp had enough shit out to get them. He didn't want to be part of the list.

"We're gonna have to move out of here, and soon," he said. "This is a good time to get yourselves fixed up as best you can with that first aid kit. Those of you that don't need much should gather things like water and tools and anything else we could use for shelter or protection. I'd help you, but I think it's best I supervise until you come to grips with my intentions."

The Jersey Shore kid without the busted hand said, "What happens if we don't leave? You going to shoot us?"

Rooster could tell the kid was trying to be brave, but the slight quiver in his voice gave him away. It wasn't a challenge. He was just scared and wanted to know if he should pull out his rosary beads.

"I'm not going to do anything. The gators who have been nesting in all this sawgrass, however, will do plenty. They're out in the water now, but you can bet those fuckers will be coming home soon enough. If you want to lay yourself out like an appetizer, be my guest."

He let that sink in. Now their anger at him had been replaced by fear of the gators. It was a start in the right direction.

The pilot adjusted his cap and gingerly put it back on his head. He looked left and right and sucked in hard through his teeth a few times. Finally, he said, "Man's right. I count at least a dozen nests just around us. No telling how many more are in spots I can't see."

Rooster snapped his fingers. "Okay, now that you all got a second opinion from the good pilot, I say you get your asses moving."

And move their asses did.

The girls patched up the other lady, then helped get her husband to his feet and gave him some Tylenol. The two-handed Jersey Shore was fine, except for the limp, and the little guy looked like he had just come out of the dentist and forgotten to pay the doc for his dentures.

The swarthy pilot noisily lumbered all throughout the demolished boat, ransacking every nook and cranny for supplies and things to carry them in. His head disappeared below the stern line and he got real quiet. Rooster was about to check on him, make sure he wasn't getting any funny ideas, when the blonde girl whose hair had been chopped off on the right side of her head asked him if he needed any medical attention. Her sister was luckier, the blades having given her a more even cut that made her look like a punk rocker.

"Nothing that kit can help me with," he said, feeling the burn of his ribs.

She gave a slight grin, casting her gaze downward, and walked away.

When they were done with everyone else, the girls went to the other guido, who was the worst for wear of the bunch. From the wet way he was breathing, it sounded like he had some internal bleeding. The rest went to the boat and put what supplies they could find into an old net and some shopping bags.

"How much water we got?" Rooster asked.

"Not a lot," the middle-aged guy said. He had his arm around his wife, whether to hold himself up or console her was anyone's guess. "There's six bottles of water, two bottles of Gatorade and three sodas."

We're fucked, Rooster thought. Heat like this, dehydration was going to be on them quicker than a fart through an asshole.

The pilot walked over to him. He had an old gunny sack over one shoulder and was holding a black plastic case. He said, "I don't suppose you're going to let me send up some flares."

Rooster shook his head. "Can't let that happen…yet. Why don't you hand them over before temptation gets the better of you?"

He held out his hand. The pilot thought long and hard about it, but finally slumped his shoulders and gave him the case. Rooster was glad he had come to him and asked, rather than sending one off and forcing him to put a few of these new bullets in his head.

The pilot was about to walk back to the group, paused, and said low enough for no one else to hear, "You see any sign of that monkey we run over when we came to ground?"

Rooster's first instinct was to laugh, but the man was dead serious. That head injury must have really scrambled his brains.

"What the hell are you talking about, *some monkey*? There's ain't no monkeys in the Glades."

"That's what I thought, but I saw it clear as day and even felt the boat thump it when we went over it." He looked toward the water and pointed. "In fact, I think it was standing right there."

Rooster patted his back with enough force to send him back to the others.

"Don't you go worrying about no monkeys. We got bigger problems, Mac. Why don't you help the girls get that kid on his feet?"

Fucking monkeys. Wait until thirst started settling in. The rest of them would be seeing flying giraffes and talking hippos before this day was done.

He watched everyone work together in silence, occasionally stealing glances his way. When he yawned, a family of mosquitoes got sucked in by the backdraft and lodged in his throat. His lungs went into instant convulsions and he coughed to beat the band. Stooped over, he hacked as hard as he could to get the bastards out, but it was no use.

Hocking up whatever he could, he spit into the water, hoping to expel at least one.

He stopped coughing and spitting the instant he saw the mangled lump of bloody fur and flesh curled up in a ball by the water's edge.

CHAPTER NINE

Mick saw the big guy stop and stare at something by the water. His eyes looked about ready to fall out of his skull.

"Guess I'm not so crazy after all," Mick muttered.

"Say what?" the Italian kid asked. He was busy tying a pair of Windbreakers together so he could make a sack to carry supplies in.

Mick didn't answer him. Instead, he walked over to where the big guy stood and fixed his gaze on the mangled body sitting in muddy water, blood and brain matter.

"What the hell is that?" Mick said.

"I'll tell you what it's not. That ain't no fucking monkey."

"It looks like it has two legs and two arms, but they're so tore up, it's hard to make heads or tails. Maybe if we can see the face."

Mick found an old, gnarled stick and used it to try to turn the body over. It had been squished into the mud and sand, neither wanting to give up their desperate hold. When it came loose with a sickening burp, the foulest odor he had ever had the displeasure of smelling exploded out of the carcass.

"If I had anything in my stomach, it would be on the floor right now," Mick said, pinching his nose shut. "Feel free to get as close as you want, mister. That's as far as I care to look."

"Name's Rooster," he replied. "Mister is for old men and fags. Here, give me that stick. I want to get a better view."

"Be my guest," Mick said, backing up and shifting upwind.

Rooster worked the stick back and forth like a pry bar until the body completely turned over.

"Guess it's true," Rooster said. "The grass isn't always greener on the other side. Looks like it head-butted the boat. No telling what it looked like before it became swamp kill. But I'll tell you one thing, I've watched enough animal shows to know that ain't no monkey. A full-grown chimp, maybe, but I never seen one with such long hair. I have no fucking clue what it could be."

"Oh, my God, that's gross!" One of the girls had come over to see what the fuss was about. Mick tried to gently guide her away with a hand on her shoulder, but she wouldn't budge. Aside from the grisly body, he thought it only right to keep the girls away from their hijacker. There was no telling what was going on in his head. "Did we hit that?"

"Pretty hard," Mick said.

A long, dark shadow crept over them, turning the day to dusk in seconds. Mick looked up at the sky and shook his head.

"Afternoon storm's coming in right on time."

"Good. At least it'll cool us off and get these damn mosquitoes to quit biting us."

"Not that simple," Mick said. "The rain won't last long, and then you'll be soaked with no way to dry off in this humidity. The mosquitoes will be back when it's over, and in full force."

No sooner had he said the words than a crack of thunder signaled the downpour to follow. The rain came down in a frenzy, with no buildup. One second they were dry, the next it was like the angels were dumping truckloads of water on their heads.

Everyone started to move toward the trees, some quicker than others depending on the severity of their injuries. The one Italian kid just lay on the sand, taking the storm full in the face.

"Stay outta the damn trees!" Rooster yelled over the rumble of thunder and roar of the rain. "You don't know what's in there waiting for a fool like you to walk right in. Unless you're that witch from *The Wizard of Oz*, a little rain won't hurt you."

Mick was shocked. He realized that if Rooster (*did he really say his name was Rooster?*) wanted to get rid of them, the last thing he would do is warn them about going places that could get them killed and out of his hair.

But he did still hold on to his guns.

So they stood away from the trees and the metal boat, riding out the deluge. The sun had been obliterated and it was almost as dark as night. Mick knew these storms were as short-lived as they were vicious, but it was unnerving nonetheless.

He jumped when he heard the scream. The sudden movement brought a fireworks display to his cracked skull.

When he tried to steady himself with the girl, he saw that she had grabbed hold of Rooster's arm.

Now everyone was screaming, most of all the Italian kid who couldn't stand.

Something big was dragging him off, and it didn't sound happy.

Rooster had perfect eyesight, but he still couldn't make out the tall, broad figure through the wall of rain and gloom. It had to be a man, and one hell of a big one at that. If Rooster was right, it was over seven feet tall, if not eight. It was hard to tell with it all hunched down, wrangling the kid.

"Noooo! Noooo! Noooo! Somebody help me!" the Italian kid bawled.

He was being lugged away from them by the ankle. He clawed at the sand in a futile attempt to halt his progress into the total darkness beyond the trees.

"Angelo!" his buddy shouted, running over to help.

Rooster was suddenly hit by an overwhelming odor that made the ball of mess in the water smell like potpourri. It was like a combination of gasoline, body odor, wet dog and the inside of a baby's diaper. Everyone else must have smelled it, too, because he saw a lot of crinkled noses.

Suddenly, there was a loud roar, like what Rooster would imagine a tiger caught in a bear trap would sound like, that turned the piss in his bladder to ice.

And it was coming from the thing carting the kid off.

The kid's friend was almost on top of him, and there was another roar, followed by a hard slap, and the kid went down like Tyson had given him an uppercut.

Rooster pulled the gun from his belt and cocked the hammer back.

A pair of red eyes cut through the murk, pausing for a moment on each one of them, taking them in, daring someone to make a move.

He took a few, slow steps forward, refusing to blink despite the irritating rivulets of water burning his eyes. The girl kept by his side.

"Oh shit," Rooster hissed.

That wasn't no man holding the kid.

He couldn't recall any man being over seven feet tall *and* covered with hair. Its hair was long and matted, and he realized the awful stink was coming off of it in repulsive waves. There was a small, hairless patch of what looked to be rough, sun-scorched skin just around the nose, eyes and mouth. But those eyes. Dear God, it was like looking into the eyes of Satan himself!

"Let me go!" the kid shouted, breaking the stare-down. He tried to kick the beast with his free leg, but it twisted his body with the ease of flicking a jump rope, causing him to miss badly. There was a loud crunch and the kid wailed so hard, Rooster thought his throat would burst.

"Was that his ankle?" the girl whispered.

Rooster nodded. He sure as shit couldn't think of any man who could crush another man's bones like that.

"Shoot it," the girl said.

He didn't need to be told twice. Rooster raised the gun and squeezed the trigger. The gun went off at the exact same time as a flash of lightning lit up their world, temporarily blinding him. When he opened his eyes, the beast and the Italian kid were gone.

A swath of sawgrass waved from side to side, the fading sign of the monster's quick escape. The only sound was the pounding of the rain on the water and the long, heavy leaves of the trees.

How did I miss it? There was no way it could have ducked his shot. Nothing on earth was that fast. Nothing.

He looked down at the girl. "Stay right here."

Everyone else was huddled together by the wrecked boat. Rooster strode over to where the other kid lay, keeping his gun well out in front. His finger applied enough pressure on the trigger to make the gun go off with the slightest provocation. Bending down on one knee next to the kid, but keeping his eyes on the tree line where the monster had taken off, he gave him a soft slap on the cheek. The kid answered with a dull moan.

"You good enough to get up?" Rooster asked. His guts were pulled tight and his nose wanted to call it quits. The smell was even worse here.

"I...I think so."

"Then do it quick. It ain't safe here. I'll help you."

He lifted him with his free arm and walked backward to the rest of the group.

The relentlessness of the rain eased up, signaling the beginning of the storm's end. Less than a minute later, it had passed, leaving them soaked, confused and frightened. And true to Mick's word, the heat came back with a vengeance, as did the mosquitoes.

"Anybody got a fucking clue what the hell that was?" Rooster said. His head swiveled in every direction, waiting for it to reappear. His heart was beating so hard he thought it was going to turn his rib cage to dust.

All heads turned when the little guy stammered, "I think I do, but I sure do hope I'm wrong."

PART TWO
FRIGHT

CHAPTER TEN

"My name's Jack Campos. I was just taking a break from a conference, wanted to get a chance to see firsthand what the Everglades were like, you know? All I expected to see were some alligators and birds. You all might think I'm crazy, but I've seen that *thing* before." Because of his missing teeth, he whistled a good deal of the words.

Everyone had gathered in a circle around him. Jack wasn't used to being the center of attention, and their incredulous looks weren't making things any easier for him.

As he struggled to find the right words to say, the man with the gun said, "I find it hard to believe that anyone has ever seen anything like that before."

Jack cleared his throat. "Now, I…I didn't say I had ever seen one with my own eyes. Don't get me wrong on that. What I am saying is that I've heard about that particular creature and saw some artist renditions and a few grainy photographs. I'm a—" He paused. "I've always been fascinated by cryptozoology. If I thought I could make a living off of it, I would have traded in my desk job a long time ago. Plus, I have a nephew, Tobi, who's really into all that paranormal stuff. He's got good reasons to be. Kid's got gifts." He lost himself for a moment, thinking about Tobi, then shook his head. "Being his favorite uncle, I get exposed to a lot of it."

"What the heck is cryptozoology?" one of the pretty blonde girls asked.

"It's the study of animals that have yet to be discovered. Most people call them monsters, like the kinds of things you hear about in myths and legends," the middle-aged man answered. Now all eyes were on him. "I like to watch those crazy shows on the History Channel. Name's John, by the way, and this is my wife, Carol. Since we're all going to be together for the foreseeable future, probably makes sense to know each other's names." He pulled his wife closer to him, and she gave a weak hello.

The guy with the gun raised his hand. "Before this turns into an AA meeting, I'd like to let Jack here finish what he was saying. Now, you said you knew what that was. Spill it."

Jack's heart palpitated when he looked into the man's hard, cold eyes. A torrent of sweat seeped from every pore. Incompetent marketing managers he could deal with. This guy was way out of his league.

"Well, from what I could see, combined with that terrible odor, I think what we just saw was a skunk ape."

The Italian kid's friend, who had been quiet and looking down until now, shouted, "You think we're gonna believe my best friend just got taken by a fucking smelly ape?" He grabbed Jack by the front of his shirt and shook him. "Give me one reason why I shouldn't kick your ass."

The barrel of the pistol slowly descended between them.

"Is this one?"

The pilot took off his hat and rubbed his bandaged head. "Shit, I've heard of skunk apes, but I thought that was just a load of crap. Far as I knew, it was just a story to scare kids from going into the woods and swamps at night."

"So this thing that dragged that kid off and dodged my bullet is part skunk and part ape? That just doesn't sound possible."

Jack shook his head. "The name is misleading. It actually has nothing to do with skunks *or* apes. The skunk part comes because of that awful stench. I suspect being a large biped in this kind of climate would lead to a certain degree of, well, stink. The term skunk ape is just a localized version of a much more well-known creature. I'm sure you've all heard of Bigfoot?"

There were a few nods, but most looked at him like he had sprouted fairy wings and a golden horn from his forehead. He patted his messenger bag.

"I'd show you more about skunk apes and Bigfoot on my laptop, but something tells me I'm not going to get a Wi-Fi connection out here. There's this podcast called the Paranormal Podcast. Guy called Jim Harold has interviewed folks about the skunk ape. It's really fascinating stuff."

One of the girls turned to the pilot and the thug and asked, "You think it's related to that?"

Her head turned to an area near the water.

"Mind if I see what *it* is?" Jack asked.

"Sure. Come with me." Walking behind her, he could catch the fading odor of her perfume, a welcome relief. One side of her hair had been hacked to hell, but she still made it look good. A mosquito tried to wriggle up his nose, and he almost broke it trying to slap the annoyance away.

She turned to him and said, "I'm Maddie. My sister back there is Liz."

"Nice to meet you, Maddie," Jack said, then added, "well, as nice as it can be under the circumstances."

"I'm going to warn you, it's pretty grisly."

She fixed him with her gaze and he straightened as best he could. He'd seen that look countless times before. Just because he was small in stature didn't mean he couldn't handle the ugly parts of life.

"I'll be fine," he said, and moved past her.

She was right. It *was* grisly. The furry body looked like it had been tossed in a man-sized blender and put through the chop cycle for ten seconds.

"You might want this," Maddie said, handing him the stick the pilot had used before.

Jack poked and prodded, not even noticing that everyone else had come down to watch. Everyone but the Italian kid.

It smelled rancid. Blood-soaked hair covered every square inch of it. Definitely looked like a pair of legs, and there was a fleshy area that could have been a hand.

He gave a start when he turned and saw the group was just inches from his back.

"If I saw this alone, I wouldn't try to attempt to classify it, but, when you add in what just happened, I'd definitely say it looks, and smells, like a skunk ape. A young one at that."

Maddie's sister, Liz, moved in closer.

"Are you saying we ran over a Bigfoot baby?" she said, bending at her knees to get as near as she could without getting into the tainted water.

The pilot looked back at where the kid had been taken. "If that's true, then we have one pissed-off momma Bigfoot on our hands."

"Skunk ape or Bigfoot or not, we can't stay here and wait for it to come back," Rooster said. "Before you all attacked me and sent this boat to shitsville, I was fixing to get to my father's safe house. Last I remember, he had a ham radio and crank generator, and usually canned food and water. The food and water are probably spoiled by now, but the radio is the key. I'd guess it's about another five miles north of here, which ain't gonna be easy to navigate on foot."

He left out how unsafe it would be, seeing as they were flipped out enough. Folks had been hiding out in the Glades for centuries. It was still one of the best places on the planet to up and disappear into. Even if they didn't find his father's rickety old cabin, they might come across another. Hopefully it would be one without a hostile hermit in residence with a penchant for shooting trespassers.

"You know how to get there without a boat? It's not the same as navigating through the water channels," the pilot said.

Rooster asked, "What do they call you, Mac?"

"Mick. It's short for Michael."

Putting a hand on the pilot's bulky shoulder, Rooster said, "It's either that, or sit here like a corn dog on a dinner plate. I've got a pretty good sense of direction, and I'd like to get our asses moving before nightfall, while I still have the sun to help me with my direction." He unzipped the duffel bag of guns and showed the contents to everyone. "Now, I'm not saying you have to come with me. To be honest with you, I'm sorry I got you stuck out here, but I can't take all the blame." He took a moment to look them each in the eye. "All I *can* do is try to get us somewhere safe. Seeing as none of us are in any kind of shape to go *mano a mano* with a swamp ape…"

"*Skunk* ape," Jack interrupted, looking immediately regretful.

"Skunk ape sounds stupid," Rooster said with a dismissive wave of his hand. "I'm calling it a Bigfoot from now on. Anyway, I have enough pistols in here for everyone. Problem is, I don't have enough bullets to fill them, but you'll each have a few shots, should you need 'em."

They eyed the bag of guns, then him, deciding whether it was a test or not. Sighing, he reached in, grabbed a handful and put one in each of their reluctant hands. Even the upset Italian kid came over to get his piece. When he went to take it, Rooster tightened his grip. He whispered to him, "I know you're upset about your friend, but something about you tells me I have to add a little word of caution. Trust me when I say, I have far more experience when it comes to firearms, and lifetimes more when it comes down to killing a man. You use this to protect yourself from anything that *ain't* human and out to get you. Do we understand one another?"

Rooster gently placed it in his palm. The kid hefted it a bit, surprised by its weight. Most people who'd never handled a gun before were.

"All I want," the kid said, "is to get that fucking thing that took Angelo."

"Which way is it to your father's house?" John asked, breaking the tension.

Rooster pointed in the direction where the Bigfoot had slipped away.

"You have got to be fucking kidding me," the girl with the half-Mohawk said.

All Rooster could do was shake his head. "Afraid not, sister."

"We're not your sisters," the other one said. "We prefer Liz and Maddie." She made a pinching motion and a phantom pain crept into his arm.

"Beg your pardon," he said sarcastically. For all his bravado, he did not want to get in her grip again.

Liz turned to the Italian kid and said, "Hey, maybe Angelo is still alive. At least this way, we have a chance of finding him. Your name's Dominic, right? I thought I heard your friend say that back on the dock. I'm going with you guys."

The afternoon sun was making Rooster dizzy. He had to get them moving fast.

"Show of hands, who wants to stay here?"

To his surprise, none went up, but there was serious doubt in a lot of eyes.

Mick said, "We're sitting ducks out here, and where there's shelter, there's safety."

Carol said, "We could light a fire and wait for a rescue party to find us."

"Everything around us is soaked. I doubt you'd be able to start a fire with a can of kerosene out here," Maddie said.

Everyone gave a start when a high-pitched howl echoed across the swamp. It didn't sound exactly like the Bigfoot from before, but it didn't sound like any other kind of animal either.

"I think that pretty much decided it for us," Jack said.

"Smart. Here, everyone load four, five for the ladies, into your gun and pass it around," Rooster said, tossing the box of bullets to Maddie. She caught it with one hand, loaded the chambers and gave it a spin. Nice.

"At least when we get in the trees, we'll be out of the sun for a bit. The less you sweat, the better off you'll be. Grab those supplies and let's go."

CHAPTER ELEVEN

The early going wasn't easy, what with the razor-sharp sawgrass making mincemeat of their legs. They followed the trail of blood and rank odor of the skunk ape until both evaporated into the cloying atmosphere. Liz hoped that Rooster's shot had been true and the blood, or at least the majority of it, belonged to the beast.

The constant attack of mosquito hordes was getting on Liz's last nerve. She'd slapped herself silly trying to squish their damned little bodies. It was important to her that they try to find Angelo. Her father had been a Marine, and he always taught her to never leave a man behind, even if you hated his guts. Enemy hands were no place to leave a fallen man. And the skunk ape was most certainly their enemy.

"What I wouldn't do for some bug repellant," she said, wending her way around a cypress tree.

Carol, who was right behind her, said, "I had some in my bag but it got crushed. I wonder how many bites a person can take before they start to have some kind of reaction." There was heavy concern in her voice.

"Guess we'll find out soon enough," Jack said. He slipped on a clump of moss and almost took a header.

John reached forward to stop him. "You gotta watch yourself, guy."

Jack's face flushed red and he continued on, this time with his eyes on the ground.

The sound of rapid-fire knocking on a tree froze everyone in their tracks. Liz heard Jack mutter to himself, "Tree knocking is one of the ways they communicate with one another over long distances."

Mick said, "It's fine. Just a woodpecker. The things you have to worry about are on the ground. Especially watch out for snakes. Lot of copperheads, rattlers and king snakes in these parts. If you get bit, there's no saving you."

"Aren't you supposed to suck out the poison?" Carol asked.

"Only if the person doing the sucking wants to die along with you," Mick replied, and resumed walking.

Liz felt rivers of sweat cascading down into crevices of her body that should not be wading pools. Each inhalation felt like she was sucking fire through a damp cloth. She desperately wanted a drink, but knew it was too soon to dip into their supplies.

She heard a splash up ahead, and knew things were about to get worse.

Rooster came to the end of the line and inspected the water, searching for gator eyes resting on the surface. The next landmass was about hundred yards north, which meant they were going to have to have to get in the water, where God-only-knew-what could be waiting.

Maddie, being less cautious, jumped right in before he could stop her.

"Oh, man, that's refreshing!" she said. "I thought I was going to melt."

She dipped down to her neck, and when she rose up from the water, her thin shirt had gone translucent, revealing her white bra and a set of very hard, wide nipples underneath that. Rooster swallowed hard. She looked so damn good, he was tempted to jump in and wrap his arm around her waist just so he could feel those puckered points against his chest and hold her, cheek to cheek. Most of the women he'd been around had lived hard lives. Birds of a feather. He'd never been this close to someone like Maddie before. If there was a silver lining to this shit cloud they were under, this was it.

Instead, he held his hand out to her. "Quick, get out before you stir something up. And keep your gun out of the water."

She grasped his hand and let him pull her out.

"I'm sorry. It just looked so good."

"That's an illusion. There're all kinds of alligators and snakes in there that'll ruin your day, not to mention the turtles. If they get a hold of you with those beaks, they're leaving with a pound of your flesh."

Dominic caught up to them and knelt at the water's edge, pushing fallen leaves around. He got excited and jumped up. "Look! There's blood on this one. We must be right behind them."

Rooster plucked the leaf from his hand and brought it up to his nose. He recoiled from the smell. "Yep, that's from them all right. Looks like we're all headed the same way."

Finding Angelo was the least of Rooster's concerns, but he had to play the game to keep everyone with him. Knowing that some crazed Bigfoot or whatever it could be was out there changed the game. Rooster needed numbers, especially when they all had guns. Getting out of this mess alive meant depending on the group.

"Mick, come up here!" Rooster hollered.

The pilot was deathly pale. Blood had mixed with his sweat so he looked like an extra from a horror movie.

"I need a second pair of eyes. You see anything between here and that spot?" He pointed to the horseshoe-shaped landmass slightly to their right.

Mick squinted, taking his time, while Rooster gave another sweep of their immediate area, which was where most of the bad shit would lie in wait.

"It looks clear to me, but you know there could be anything under the surface."

"Yeah, I know, but we'll have to take our chances." He turned to the group. "We're heading for that island over there. Odds are the water will be pretty shallow, so hopefully we can walk across. But you may have to swim in parts. Keep your gun over your head. If it gets wet, it's about as useful as a rock. I'll take the lead, and Mick here will stay in the middle. Liz, you seem like you can handle yourself. You opposed to taking the rear?"

The girl quietly shook her head.

Mick added, "And watch out for gator holes. When the water's low, they dig these big old holes looking for food. Now that the water's high, you can't see them until you drop in one. Just be ready to tread water if your foot comes across empty space."

That seemed to rattle a few cages. Mick noticed and added, "The gators aren't *in* the holes now. Just be aware that you may come across some deep pits."

"No sense lugging this around," Rooster said. He dropped the bag of guns, which only had five more, and hung it on a branch. "If I'm lucky, I can come back for this later."

"What about that small one?" Maddie asked, nodding toward the tool bag of money.

He just smiled and left it at that.

"Good. Let's get wet."

Rooster eased into the water and had to admit that Maddie was right. Despite the ball-shriveling fear that something in the murk was moments from biting or eating him, the cool water did wonders for chasing the heat stroke away.

He heard Dominic say, "Angelo's probably over there too, right?"

When Rooster turned, he saw John and Carol put a hand on each of his shoulders. "I'm sure he is," Carol said.

Dominic jumped in like a kid at a public pool, anxious to find his friend. Next was Mick. He filled his cap with water and let it rain down over his head, washing the blood off his face. Jack came in tentatively after him, his eyes wide and searching for imminent death.

Maddie and Rooster had gone about twenty yards and the water was still chest high, at least for him. They hopped on the balls of their feet, moving ahead steadily. A breeze had picked up and was at their backs. It felt good.

But it also carried something with it.

"Oh shit!"

Rooster spun around and shouted, "Get in the water, now!"

Liz, John and Carol were still on land, tying one of the supply bags to John's back. They must have smelled it, too, because each of them stopped and stiffened.

Instantly, the mangrove trees came alive with unearthly wailing that would freeze a man's piss midstream.

What came bursting out of them would haunt Rooster until the day he died.

CHAPTER TWELVE

John felt the hammer blow to his back before he had a chance to turn around. It sounded like a herd of stampeding wildebeests.

He hit the shallow water face-first and got a mouth full of gunk from the bottom. When he exploded to the surface, he couldn't help but scream.

Four hairy monsters, the smallest at just about seven feet, the largest over eight, stood side by side on the shore, bellowing with murderous intent. All had broad, muscular chests, and one sported a pair of drooping, furred breasts. The hair on their heads was long, like an 80s glam band gone rogue. Their immense, talon-like hands hung low, almost to their knees. A small amount of bronze flesh was visible on their faces, but the rest of them just looked like bipedal woolly mammoths. And their eyes! Eight flaming eyes bored out from under all that hair and filth.

"Carol!"

Liz was nowhere to be seen, but three of the skunk apes had hold of his wife. Tears ran down her face and she wailed, "John! Please, help me!"

He whipped around to see Rooster take a careful shot at the one that held Carol's left arm. A jet of blood sprouted from its shoulder, but it didn't let go.

Instead, it tightened its grip, bringing out a scream from Carol that didn't seem humanly possible.

"It's breaking my arm!" she shouted.

John fought the mire that tried to hold him in place. He was weeping and shouting and out of his mind with helpless anger and fear.

"Just hold on, baby!"

He was inches from shore when the beasts bent at the knees in a concerted effort and tugged. Carol came apart in three shredded hunks as easily as a cheap piñata. One of them held a portion that contained her right leg, part of her torso, neck, and worst of all, still-screaming head.

"Nooooooo!"

John meant to empty every bullet he had in his gun, but it had been lost in the water.

Another shot rang out, biting off the trunk of a tree.

He heard someone shout, "John, get back!"

Carol's eyes settled on his, and her shouting, and her pain, stopped. A final tear snaked down her cheek, and she was silent.

The skunk apes tossed her pieces into the water, beating at the ground with their massive hands and screeching, baring jagged, yellow teeth.

A hand grabbed John's shoulder and pulled him away. It was Jack. Dazed, John went limp and allowed himself to be trailed along like a floatable pool toy. His stomach heaved and he threw up.

Carol.

He couldn't save her.

Please forgive me! I failed you when you needed me most!

He blocked out the impossible horror on the shore. He could only see the final, pleading moment in Carol's eyes.

Jack, pulling John, passed Dominic, who had squared his legs and shoulders and was deciding which skunk ape to shoot.

"You motherfuckers!"

He pulled the trigger and the pistol jerked up, missing high and wide.

"Save your bullets!" Rooster shouted. He had come back and was right behind him. "They're too far for you."

He was right. Dominic needed to go to *them.*

"Are you crazy?" Rooster hollered. He felt the big man's fingers swipe at his neck and shoulder but shrugged them off.

Dominic advanced to the shore. His heart thundered in his chest. These amped-up gorillas had taken Angelo and killed that lady. He wasn't going to run away. They had to pay.

The skunk apes stopped their ungodly howling and trained their attention on him. They mustn't have been used to having prey come *to* them. Odds were, they were the king shits out here. But alligators and bears and panthers didn't have guns, and they weren't from the Bronx.

"You think you're tough shit?" Dominic cried out. He smiled when he saw the river of blood running down one of their arms. "You sure as hell aren't bulletproof."

He picked the huge one with the chest that looked like it was made of two beer kegs, aimed at its heart and shot.

The skunk ape darted to the side with the dexterity of a gazelle, and the bullet impotently sailed into the trees.

"How…how did it do that?"

"We'll figure it out later, kid," Rooster hissed, yanking him away and into deeper water.

And that's when the fourth skunk ape, relegated to the shadows, came sprinting out from behind a twisted mangrove tree, holding a headless body high above its head.

Oh no! Angelo!

It launched Angelo's body at them, slamming into Dominic and Rooster like the world's heaviest medicine ball. They both went under from the impact. When Dominic struggled to get air, his hand errantly reached into the open cavity of Angelo's neck, dipping his fingers deep into his best friend's frayed innards. The last of his air burst from his lungs, and he kicked and pumped his arms until he was free.

He came up just in time to hear three quick shots. The skunk apes turned to their right and skittered away.

Liz had popped up from behind the roots of a mangrove, her pistol blazing.

The skunk apes shrieked, but it sounded more like fear than fury. They ran in a pack in the opposite direction and took to the water, splashing and making more noise than an old outboard motor. Liz followed them to the shoreline, emptying her last bullet into the white froth that the monsters had kicked up.

As suddenly as the madness had started, it was over. The skunk apes went under water and didn't come back up. There weren't even bubbles on the surface to betray the direction they had gone.

Angelo's body bobbed against Dominic.

He looked down at what was left of his friend, and felt all of his defenses crumble. For the first time since he was a little kid, he wept.

CHAPTER THIRTEEN

They made it to the next island without any further surprises. Rooster figured the good Lord had had enough amusement with them, at least for the moment.

A royal palm tree made a good leaning post and offered shade from the relentless sun. Everyone was winded, soaked to their taints and scared. Rolling to his side, Rooster rummaged around one of the bags of supplies and opened a bottle of water.

"You all take a sip and pass it around. Leave enough to go around." He took the first pull and had to stop himself from chugging it down. His body cried out for more, his stomach cramping. Instead, he wiped the top and passed it to Jack.

He looked over at John, who sat with his forearms over his knees, staring at the ground like he was looking into the center of a black hole. Poor bastard had checked out. Rooster couldn't blame him. He'd seen a lot of bad shit go down in his life, but what had happened to Carol beat them all to hell. The way they ripped her apart, it was like watching a couple of little kids tearing a sheet of paper, except with blood spraying in every direction and internal organs slopping to the ground in a piping pile.

Dominic, on the other hand, looked like a penned-in bull waiting to enter the ring. He didn't cry long, and Rooster had to physically restrain him from dragging Angelo's body along with them. The way he saw it, that body would distract all the predators in the area, keep them away from those who still had heads.

"Anyone see which way they went?" Mick asked.

Liz answered, "It looked like they went for that other island over there, I'd say two hundred yards east of us. At least that's the direction they started in."

"It's like they were fish," Jack said. "Skunk apes are land mammals. How could they swim that great a distance without coming up for air?"

"You ever study a skunk ape to see how it swims?" Maddie asked.

Jack's eyebrow rose. "That's crazy. No one has."

"Exactly, so no one knows what those things are capable of," she shot back. She stabbed a stick repeatedly into the ground between her feet.

Jack was quiet for a moment, then said, "It would make sense that something that large would have considerably sized lungs. Maybe they've adapted to living in the Everglades so they can hold air longer, seeing as there's so much water in the environment and being under the water is safer than above. It keeps them in a predatory position."

Rooster picked up the empty water bottle and tossed it at Jack's head. "No one gives a shit, Einstein. We got to get up and get moving. Night'll be coming soon, and I don't want to leave my ass exposed like this. Further we go into the interior, the better chance we have to find a secluded spot."

He counted the guns that were left to them. Six.

"How many bullets you all have left?" he said.

They each opened the chamber.

"I'm all out," Liz said.

"Thought you would be," he said. The way that girl came charging out of the woods like Annie Oakley and that chick from *Alien* was damn impressive. He removed two of the four bullets he had left and tossed them to her. "Don't wanna leave you empty."

She smiled and loaded them up.

"I've got two," Dominic said, looking at him like he was the bullet fairy.

"I still have four," Jack said.

"Me, too," Mick chimed in. "You can have one of mine, kid. And Jack, you look like you could use another. Something tells me once you start pulling the trigger, you're not stopping. "

Or hitting anything, Rooster thought.

.

"Okay, that means you all can only pull your trigger if you have a clear, close shot. There're at least four of them out there, and it didn't look like that one bullet even fazed the one I plugged. They're fucking fast, so the more distance between them and you means the more likely they'll dodge your shot. You're gonna have to wait until they're almost on you. Everyone understand?"

All heads nodded, except John's.

"All right, let's start hauling ass."

He held out his hand to help Maddie to her feet. Her hand was soft but there was a lot of strength there. Liz approached them and said, "What are we going to do about him?" She nodded at immobile John. The man was a vegetable.

"I'll get the kid to help me with him. You two take the lead. One of you keep an eye on the ground for snakes, the other to the sides and forward in case our friends show up. There's lots of natural lean-tos out here. If we find one a good distance from the water, we stop."

They nodded and started walking through more sawgrass. Their legs looked like they had traipsed through a herd of raging cats, but they didn't so much as wince when the sharp blades cut through existing wounds.

"Hey, Jersey, help me take a side so we can get going."

Dominic didn't look happy to be on babysitting duty, but he did what he was told.

They walked through the palm and mangroves, taking deep breaths to detect if the Bigfoots were near. Rooster's eyes stung from sweat, and more than once he was tempted to dump John's deadweight, if only to relieve some of his own pain. His ribs were killing him. But Dominic stayed strong, and he'd be damned to give up before some punk kid.

Jack was blathering on about what little he knew about skunk apes, from what they ate (fish and plants) to his theories on whether or not they could build and use tools. It was nothing but nervous chatter, and none of it seemed the least bit useful. All that hot air made Rooster's head spin.

Finally, Mick turned to Jack with narrowed eyes and said, "Can you please shut up?"

He did.

And then they heard the shot.

CHAPTER FOURTEEN

Rooster and Mick darted to the girls with their guns at the ready.

"You girls okay?" Rooster said.

Maddie waved a hand. "We're fine. Liz stepped on that sucker's tail. I didn't want to give him a chance to retaliate."

Mick whistled. "Holy shit. That's one of the biggest cottonmouths I've ever seen."

The bullet had caught the snake three inches below its head, severing it from its long, coiled body. It had to be almost five feet long.

Rooster patted her on the shoulder. "Nice shot. You still cool with taking point?"

"Hell yeah. That was a good idea you had about one set of eyes on the ground. Just saved at least one of our lives," she said.

He went back to helping Dominic carry John, and she and Liz kept moving forward. Long, ominous shadows had begun to seep in among the trees, and the sun slunk down over the horizon. They had to find someplace relatively safe fast, but so far all they had found were trees and old leaves. There were some sweet bay bushes, waist high and looking like little trees, but they could barely conceal a squirrel.

The constant thrumming of tree frogs grew as night approached. Maddie thought it sounded nice, kind of peaceful, which was a welcome thing right about now. She was so glad Liz was still by her side and unharmed. And in a weird way, she was thankful to have Rooster with them, even if it was mostly his fault they were stuck out here. She had been taught to be self-sufficient, but there was a simmering power in him that she knew they'd need to get out alive. She also suspected that he wasn't as bad as he'd like people to think. It didn't hurt that physically, he was right in her sweet spot.

Jesus, Maddie, get a grip! she scolded herself. *Way to moon over a bad boy like a dumb teen.*

"You think we're going to make it out of here?" she asked Liz. They may have been identical in appearance, but Liz had always been the stronger and smarter one. Must have been because Liz was born five minutes ahead of her. Liz had the advantage of more life experience.

Liz squeezed her arm. "I don't *think* so, no. I *know* we are."

When Maddie turned to thank her, she saw, over her sister's shoulder, where they would hole up for the night.

"I think you're right."

Night chased the sun's brutal rays away, but the humidity increased to the point where it felt like they were underwater.

Everyone was exhausted. The fallen mahogany tree made a good place to stay and provided ample protection to their backs. It would have been nice to light a fire, but no one had matches or a lighter, not that any of the tinder would have held a flame. Besides, they didn't want to betray their position to the murderous Bigfoots.

They decided that two people would take watch at a time. Rooster chose Maddie to sit first watch with him. He saw her sister's reproachful glare, so he explained to her that he needed someone good with a gun on each watch. It didn't look like she bought it, but she was too tired to argue.

Liz, Jack, Mick and Dominic slept shoulder to shoulder against the trunk. John sat apart from them, his eyes half open, though whether he was conscious or not was anyone's guess.

Rooster and Maddie stood against a nearby mangrove, searching the darkness for any sign of encroachment.

"I figure we'll smell 'em before we see 'em," he said to her.

"Unless they're smart enough to stay downwind of us. Something that big would need a lot of food, and I don't think Jack's theory of them eating fish and berries holds water. If you ask me, they know how to hunt, and they know how to hunt *big game*. There's lots out here to choose from. That would also mean they've learned how to sneak up on their prey undetected."

"They teach you shit like that in college?" he asked.

She let out a small laugh. "Nah. Liz and I grew up in a military family. Our daddy taught us all kinds of stuff about hunting and survival. You may not think so, but we were a couple of total tomboys growing up. We knew how to make traps, throw knives and defend ourselves from personal attack before we hit our teens."

"After the number you did on me on the boat, I could tell your daddy that he did a good job."

Heat lightning flickered in the sky. There was no thunder, and thankfully, no rain. The lightning offered brief glimpses of their immediate area, and all was quiet, save for the droning of the frogs and buzzing of the mosquitoes.

Maddie sighed. "He died a year ago yesterday. He'd always wanted to see the Everglades. That's why Liz and I came down here. We were kind of hoping he'd see it right along with us."

That hurt. Rooster's moment of rage had taken them from grief to running for their lives. He was about to apologize when she said, "You mind telling me why you have a bags of guns and money and why those guys were trying to kill you? I'm not being nosy, but you just don't seem the gun-running type."

"And you know what the gun-running type looks like?"

"I watch a lot of movies and reality cop shows."

He swatted a family of flies off his neck. "Long story short?"

She nodded.

"I wasn't exactly running guns. These were for my collection. I'm a big Shooter Jennings fan. You know, the country singer? Waylon's son?"

"I've heard of him. Who's Waylon?"

Rooster was shocked, but had to remind himself that she was young. "Anyway, these pistols look just like the one Shooter has tattooed on his arm. I heard through the grapevine that this guy Cheech in the Cuban mob had a box of them. I don't know why, but I just had to have them. I've dealt with Cheech on other…matters, so I figured it would be easy. I got the money by knocking off a few stores and stealing some cars. I know this may sound weird, but I was kinda hoping that I could somehow get Shooter's attention through the collection and maybe, I don't know, he'd send me a ticket to one of his shows, maybe even float me a backstage pass."

"So you *are* a bad guy. And maybe a little stalkerish on the side. You know, you could have just used that ill-gotten money to *buy* a concert ticket and backstage pass."

Lightning flashed and he could see that she wasn't the least bit afraid.

"I'm no saint, but I ain't the Devil. Come to think of it, I guess I just really wanted those guns. Anyway, I go to get them and Cheech, well, he was all fucked up and had his beer balls on, started ragging on me. It got to the point where I had to shut him up and he kinda died."

"You killed him?"

"It was an accident. I only punched him a couple of times. I guess coke does all kinds of weird shit to your skull, because his head caved right in. Then his cronies found me and the body, and I took off. The rest you know."

They stood in silence and Rooster figured she was taking everything in. After a while, she asked, "What did he say to make you kill him?"

"Accidentally," he added.

"Yes, *accidentally*."

This was the hard part. How else could he say it without sounding like an insecure kid in a school yard? Might as well rip the Band-Aid off and suck it up.

"He kept making fun of my name."

"Well, you do have an odd name." She said it without a hint of sarcasm or mockery.

"My dad was a real John Wayne and Johnny Cash fan. He wanted to toughen me up like the guy in that song *A Boy Named Sue*, but instead of Sue, he called me Rooster after his favorite John Wayne film."

"I guess it worked," she said.

"Huh. Rooster Murphy. All it gave me was a lifetime of anger issues." It felt good talking to Maddie about this, way better than those therapists or his anger management coach. For the first time he could remember, he felt calm.

"I think it's a pretty cool name. Hard to forget," she said and giggled.

He jerked to his left when he heard the quick rush of leaves. Maddie reacted by raising her gun in the direction of the commotion.

Deep, angry growls filled the damp air, but it didn't sound anything like the Bigfoots.

Something heavy thumped so hard into the ground near them that it shook like a tiny earthquake. The growls grew louder and more objects crashed through the darkness.

It was during one of the sparks of lightning when Rooster saw what was piling up around them in an angry, thrashing mosh pit.

The fucking Bigfoots were throwing alligators at them!

CHAPTER FIFTEEN

"What the hell? Aaahhhhhh!"

Rooster could hear Jack screaming but he couldn't see a damn thing. He put his arm over Maddie's chest to hold her back.

He felt the ground shake again, and another angry roar echoed in the darkness.

The entire forest had erupted in gator growls, Bigfoot howls, human screams and mad scrambling. When the next flash of lightning came, it was all Rooster could do to keep from running.

Four alligators faced everyone by the collapsed tree with open jaws. A heavy, ominous rumble purred from their throats. Liz, Jack, Mick and Dominic huddled together, scrambling for their guns.

Now normally gators were pretty timid, doing what they could to avoid interaction with humans, but it appeared they took great exception to being thrown about in the dead of night.

"Don't move!" Rooster shouted. "And most of all, do not jump over to the other side of that tree. They're trying to flush us out!"

Maddie gripped his arm so hard he was sure she was drawing blood. "What's happening?"

"Those fucking apes just tossed four very angry gators at us."

If possible, her grip tightened. "Oh, my God, what do we do?"

"I'm thinking!"

His head was pounding, whether from fatigue, thirst, fear, uncertainty or all four was too hard to tell. All of the gators came from the rear side of the downed tree. The Bigfoots either wanted them to run right into their waiting arms so they could break them down like cheap Legos, or they were happy to let the gators do their dirty work. He could hear the Bigfoots howling and shuffling around. It almost sounded like they were cheering the gators on.

That was mistake number one.

Now he knew exactly where the hairy assholes were, which left them an escape route.

"Okay, we're going to have to get everyone over to us," he said, wiping the sweat from his gun hand.

"How can we do that?"

"Just sit tight and don't pull that trigger unless you know what you're shooting at. I'll be right back."

It could be suicide, but he figured the only way to get everyone free was to distract the gators so they could slip around them and away from the smelly fucks-in-waiting. It sounded like a goddamn zoo at feeding time. *Fucking Cheech.*

"Heyah!" he bellowed. The sound of his voice stopped Jack's screaming. "Now you all gotta pay attention. I'm going to get the gators to turn to me. Wait for the lightning. When you see them pointed away from you, run like hell behind me. Maddie's waiting. Run faster than you ever have in your life, 'cause these gators can sprint like a bottle rocket when they're riled up. You hear me?"

"We got you!" Liz shouted back, her voice tinged with uncertainty.

Lightning came, but all but one of the gators were still eyeing them like choice beef in a butcher shop window. And then there was John. There he sat, legs pulled up to his chest, eyeing the ground like hell hadn't broken out around him. That was going to be a problem.

He could hear the Bigfoots whooping it up and was tempted to take a wild shot in the dark and hope it hit something near and dear to them, but he had to hold his impulse in check. It was better to wait anyway. If he was lucky, he'd get a nice, clear shot during the day, when he could bury a bullet right between their red eyes.

Red eyes! That was it! During the day, it almost looked like their eyes glowed, as if there was a raging fire behind them. Could Rooster be so lucky that their eyes would give them away in the dark?

"Oh shit!"

Dominic's shout, followed by a blast of lightning, derailed his train of thought. Dominic was sitting atop the vertical trunk with his feet raised in the air. One of the gators had come in for the kill and just missed him.

The forest plunged into darkness and a shot cleaved the air.

"Don't shoot them," Rooster called out. "You'll only get 'em madder."

With that last burst of light, he had seen that the pack was turned his way, with the exception of the one trained on Dominic. It wouldn't wait long to try again, and it wouldn't miss Dominic twice.

"You all gotta go now!" he ordered. A series of flashes made it look like they were under a strobe light in a nightclub. He saw Mick grab Liz's wrist, and together they scampered around the gator to their left. Dominic walked along the tree like a trapeze artist, and as the gator leaped up to grab ahold of his thigh, he jumped, hitting the ground running. The clack of the gator's jaws slamming shut on nothing but air sounded like a pair of two-by-fours smashing together. Jack was right behind him, scrambling to get to his feet, his messenger bag cast aside. He lost his balance, bumping into John's side and sending him forward. John didn't even put his arms out to break his fall. He just went facedown and rolled to his side.

The lightning was relentless, which was to their advantage. Thunder decided to roll in, shuddering the bones in their chests, drowning out the Bigfoots.

Liz, Mick and Dominic raced past him and back to Maddie.

"John, get your ass up!" He screamed so hard he tasted blood on his tongue. Every gator was fixated on the prone man.

It would have been so easy to leave him there. Rooster had bailed out on plenty of other guys when things shit the bed. It was all part of his instinctual self-preservation skills, which had kept him alive in a line of work where people did not stick around long enough to collect social security.

"John! John!"

Dammit! The guy didn't deserve this. He hadn't deserved to see his wife die. And what would Maddie think if Rooster left him to die? For some odd reason, that mattered most.

"I'm coming for you, John!"

Rooster ran. Thunder clapped, and it sounded like the sky was breaking apart.

He had no idea how he was going to get past the gators, scoop John's deadweight off the ground and get them both out of Dodge.

All he could do right now was plow forward, even though his body and half his brain were screaming at him to go back.

When he felt the tip of a long tail under his foot, he stopped and jumped back a step. He cocked the gun back. If one of them was about to take a bite out of him, he was going to shove the gun into the soft inside of its mouth and pull that trigger until the gun was empty.

Nothing happened.

Instead, he heard what sounded like tearing fabric and a series of grunts.

The lightning returned, and his heart trip-hammered.

All four gators had formed a circle around John. The tearing sound was that of his flesh and bone being rent from his body. His head was in one of their mouths. All that showed was the very bottom of his chin. The gator flexed its jaw, and John's skull gave way like Styrofoam. Another had clamped on his side and locked on. One had pulled his arm free, and the other was gnawing on both legs.

"Do you have John?" Mick cried out behind him.

What the hell could he say? Sorry, John just became a late-night snack?

It was then that he noted the stink. It was heavy as an anvil, and close.

Flash!

Two of them were on the other side of the trunk, looking down at the carnage, just as he couldn't take his own gaze away. The big one with the breasts, the momma Bigfoot, gaped at John's dismemberment with calm satisfaction. Rooster's stomach quaked when he thought he saw the hint of a smile at the edges of its thin-lipped, grimy mouth.

CHAPTER SIXTEEN

Liz and Maddie told everyone else to just run while they went back for Rooster and John.

"We'll be right behind you!" Liz said, trying to keep herself under control. It felt like her blood was racing so fast that her veins would burst.

They ran blind until a wall of stink nearly stopped them dead.

"Oh, my God, that's bad," Maddie huffed. "Try breathing out of your mouth."

Liz did, and her diaphragm convulsed. "Great, now I can smell *and* taste them."

For the first time, Liz wondered if the skunk apes' foul smell was an offensive and defensive weapon. In this case, it was doing a good job of taking their minds off what they had to do and putting their guard down. If the smell was this bad, it meant the creatures were very close, and she had to put it out of her mind.

"Rooster, where are you?" Maddie cried.

Liz had the wind knocked out of her as something large and heavy collided with her side, sending her sprawling. She struggled to regain her grip on her gun. She was not going to go down without a fight.

When the hammer clicked back, she heard, "Don't shoot. It's me, Rooster! Come on, we gotta haul ass!"

Rooster grabbed under her armpit and lifted her like she weighed two pounds.

"Where's John?" she asked.

"He didn't make it. Gators."

"What about the skunk apes?" Maddie asked, panting.

"At least two are right behind us. Go!"

He stayed at their backs while they sprinted, arms and legs pumping with stores of energy that were quickly being depleted. Liz prayed that they wouldn't stumble into or hit any trees. They were one misstep away from disaster.

Maddie pulled ahead and shouted, "Guys, run!"

They had caught up to Mick, Jack and Dominic, and didn't need to tell them twice to double-time it.

Liz felt heavy thuds behind them and knew the skunk apes were gaining. By the sound of things, they had to be only a few steps behind Rooster.

"Maddie, you want to try a twist and shout?"

Maddie slowed so she could get shoulder to shoulder with her.

"Are you sure?" she said.

Liz's lungs were on fire. There was no way she could keep up this pace, and she knew she wasn't alone feeling that way. They were all dehydrated, and sooner or later their legs were going to give out.

It was twist and shout or nothing.

"Either that or run ourselves out and get killed."

Maddie didn't hesitate. "I'm in."

Their father had taught them a lot of things that they had thought were weird and unnecessary growing up. If he only knew how much they appreciated, at this moment, every afternoon spent under his watchful eye, going through drills that seemed pointless. The whole world may not be coming to an end, but if they didn't do something fast, theirs was about to have the plug pulled.

One of the skunk apes bellowed. It must have sensed the kill.

"On twist," Liz commanded.

"One."

Her right knee almost buckled and she stumbled, quickly regaining her stride.

"Two."

She could hear Rooster's labored breathing, could almost feel it on the back of her neck.

"Twist!"

Liz and Maddie stopped, dropping to a knee and spinning so they were facing the oncoming skunk apes. Rooster was taken by surprise and tripped over Maddie's leg, crashing to his chest with a mighty *whump*.

Maddie screamed, "Shout!"

They started shooting, the flare from the nozzles lighting up the area around them, cordite burning the stench of the skunk apes out of their noses.

The skunk apes, startled and finding themselves hopelessly exposed, roared and tried to swat the bullets away like they were bees from a split hive. Three of them scrambled left and right, shock visible in their wide, red eyes that cut through the pitch like lasers.

The fourth one had hung back a bit and reared its head back to let out the mother of all howls. It must have been a call to retreat, because all four darted back from where they had come, their footfalls like thunder.

"What…was…that?" Rooster wheezed.

"That's called buying us some time," Liz answered. Now it was her turn to reach out and help *him* up. "We better take advantage of it."

It was just before dawn when they stopped running (barely jogging was more like it), and came to the end of the island. They were going to have to swim over to the next one. Dominic felt something burning on his ankle and looked down to see two long, deep scratches carved into his skin. They were so deep, he thought he could see the off-white of bone beneath the tattered flesh.

"Looks like that bastard did get a piece of me," he said through shallow breaths. Everyone had collapsed around him, too tired to take another step, much less swim.

Liz looked through the remaining two supply bags and cursed. "We left the one with the first aid kit back at the tree."

Jack added wearily, "And the one with most of the food. All we have left is a couple of bottles of water and a soda" He had pulled his pants leg up and was massaging a purple golf ball in the center of his calf. One of the alligators had landed on his leg while he slept. He was lucky his leg wasn't snapped in half.

Rooster punched the ground. "We can't catch a goddamn break! Might as well pass that water around, save the rest for later when the sun gets back to baking us."

Dominic took his share and lay flat on his back. His heart was beating crazily and he couldn't get it to calm down. He'd watched three people die today. Angelo was gone. They'd known each other since freshman year in high school. Angelo had been the ultimate wing man and a true friend.

But they ripped his friggin' head off.

Mick said, "I don't think we should get in that water until light. It could only make a bad situation worse."

"Agreed," Rooster said. "Try to rest up for the next hour or so."

There were two loud splashes. Rooster had tossed the girls' guns in the water. They made no effort to protest.

"No bullets, no sense carrying them around," he said, offering Maddie his own. She held it in her lap and leaned into her sister.

Dominic reached into his pocket and tossed his over to Liz. Rooster gave him a look that, through the exhaustion, seemed a little like pride. He nodded back, then closed his eyes. He prayed for a chance at payback, even if it meant only taking one of those skunk apes straight to hell.

CHAPTER SEVENTEEN

Several quiet hours later, Mick came awake with a mouthful of mosquitoes. He spit them out with contempt, wiping and smashing their fragile bodies across the corners of his mouth and cheeks. The sun was back and he felt like he'd been sitting outside a blast furnace.

Everyone else was still asleep. Exhaustion had won out over fear. He tried to replay the events of the past twenty-four hours, but his brain wouldn't allow him to linger too long on the horrific images. The running and the terror and the heat all coalesced into a tight buzzing just under his skin. He hadn't run this much since he was a kid, and he didn't know how long his much worse-for-wear body could hold out.

Spying the bag he'd been carrying by his leg, he pulled open the clasp and silently moved next to Rooster. The big guy was propped up against a mound of sand and dirt peppered with sprouts of cattail. One of the girls—it was impossible to tell who was who—lay beside him with her arm draped across his chest.

He got close to Rooster's ear and whispered his name.

Rooster's eyes snapped open, alert, cold, dangerous. Mick swallowed hard.

"I want to show you something," he said, motioning to a spot away from the group. Rooster delicately removed the girl's arm and extricated himself. He looked remarkably refreshed, though he did wince when he tried to stretch.

"Good thing you woke me up," he said. "Time to hit the water anyway. Least it'll get these damn bugs off us for a few minutes."

"You got that right. Look, seeing as I already have a gun, I thought you should have this."

Mick pulled out a honed, shining machete and carefully handed it over.

"Where did you get this?" Rooster asked, running his thumb along the edge. A bright-red slash opened up, but he didn't react.

"I had it on the boat. I use it to hack any weeds and crap that get caught around the boat."

"Why didn't you tell us you had it?"

This was the hard part. But they were all in hell together, so there was no sense playing coy. And if he was going to be honest with himself, Mick had a strong feeling if anyone made it out of this, he wasn't going to be the one holding that winning lottery ticket. If the creatures stalking them didn't do it, dehydration would. He'd never put much stock in the saying that your body was a temple. That was sure biting him in the ass now.

He answered, "I hid it away in case I got the chance to use it on you. Before all this stuff with the skunk apes, I thought the best way out of this was to put you down. Recent events have changed my mind."

Rooster nodded. "I had you pegged for a tough guy. Truth be told, I'd have done the same thing in your shoes." He hefted it in each hand before stabbing it into the ground. "Thanks. With any luck, I'll get a chance to put it to good use."

When Jack felt a nudge in his side, he thought for sure it was one of the skunk apes and awoke scrambling, falling backward over Liz's outstretched legs. Rooster and Mick stood over him laughing. The commotion woke the others up.

"Didn't mean to make you shit yourself," Rooster said. He shook his head and tried to stifle a laugh.

"Can you blame me?" he said, more to the girls, hoping for a sympathetic ear. It seemed like everyone was amused by his overreaction. It wasn't long before he joined in the laughter. It didn't feel right to all be standing around guffawing like yokels at a *Hee Haw* convention, but he had to admit, it kinda felt good.

Mick went ankle deep in the water and splashed some on his face. "Time to get cracking. We should make it to the next island in under ten minutes. The ground is soft, so it'll be slow going."

Dominic prowled about with his head down. He grunted with primeval satisfaction when he found a palm-sized rock with a sharp point. It looked like an Indian arrowhead, if the arrow were the size of a cantaloupe.

"I wanna take point," Dominic said to Rooster.

Rooster eyed the formidable rock in his hand, then turned to Mick and said, "You mind taking point with him, since you have a gun?"

Mick nodded. Rooster said, "Jack and I will keep the girls between us. Okay, let's go."

Jack had to swallow down a yelp when he spied the ugly, fat toads that littered the edge of the water. He'd hated frogs ever since his big brother had put one in his pants at an aquarium when they were real small. Brothers had a way of instilling all kinds of lifelong fears and dislikes. He was grateful to see the toads scatter when Mick and Dominic splashed into the water.

Maddie shushed them. "Guys, try to keep it down. We don't want to give away our position."

Dominic backhanded Mick's meaty bicep. "She's right. Better take it slow."

Within five steps, the water was already up to Jack's crotch. His sac shriveled at its cool caress. Everyone walked calmly and with deliberate strides. They tried to disturb the water as little as possible. Jack's foot landed on something that quickly scrambled out from under it, and he jumped back with a loud splash.

"Come on, man," Rooster admonished him.

"Something moved under my foot. Excuse me for not being well versed in trekking through swamps."

"It was probably a turtle," Liz said. "Be glad you didn't step near its mouth."

Jack blushed. After everything they'd been through, and he couldn't imagine anyone in history having the day they'd had, he was still freaking out because a fish or a turtle or whatever was underfoot. *Stop being such a pussy, man*, he told himself.

The swamp was unnaturally quiet. It sounded and felt like all of the air had been vacuumed out. Even the ever-present mosquitoes had taken a break. It was odd not to have them caterwauling in his ears. He kept his hand with the gun above his head, not daring to get a drop of water on it. His hand trembled, as much from exhaustion as fear.

And sure enough, he stumbled into one of the gator holes. His head went under fast, but he had the presence of mind to pedal his legs and keep afloat. In seconds, he was back on squishy footing.

"Ho," Mick huffed, holding up his arm to call everyone to a stop.

"You see something?" Rooster said.

"Thought I saw bubbles coming up. Might be a gator."

All eyes were on the water ahead of Mick, waiting for the slightest disturbance on the surface. Jack realized he was holding his breath and exhaled in a head spinning rush.

No one moved.

In fact, no*thing* moved. Even the sky was free from passing hawks, herons or ospreys.

Jack's stomach cramped into a tight ball. Something was coming.

He leaned toward Rooster and whispered, "This isn't good."

Rooster flexed his grip on the machete, his eyes dead-set on the water's surface. "I know. Just be ready."

He didn't need to explain what Jack had to be ready for. Only one thing in this godforsaken swamp could make the abundant wildlife run for cover. He looked back to the island, saw the shoreline was empty. Maddie and Liz each cocked their guns. It seemed like a good idea, so Jack pulled the hammer back with his thumb and waited.

They stayed like that for several interminable minutes. The sun felt like it was sitting directly on top of his head.

The first thing to return was the chittering of the bugs. Not far behind was the cry of a bird, somewhere unseen in the trees ahead. He could see everyone's shoulders dip ever so slightly, a tiny bit of tension being released like steam from a radiator that was about to blow.

"I think we're clear," Dominic said.

Mick nodded in agreement.

They took a few, tentative steps, stopped, and when nothing happened, resumed their underwater march.

"That was weird," Maddie said.

"There had to be a predator nearby to get everything to stop like that," Jack said, an expert thanks to *Animal Planet*. "Something had to scare them off."

"Maybe it's us," Liz said. "We are the top of the food chain, and we're all carrying weapons."

Jack didn't want to remind her that the skunk apes had proven themselves to be a notch above humans on the old food-chain paradigm, and that animals and insects had no idea what guns and machetes were, hence theycouldn't fear their presence. Liz's theory seemed to make her happy, and that was good enough.

He stepped into a section of mud that sucked him down until it was up to his knee. It was a struggle to extricate his leg.

"Uh, Rooster, you think you could lend me a hand? Feels like I'm caught in quicksand."

Rooster rolled his eyes and grabbed his hand, pulling so hard he thought his shoulder would pop out of its socket.

And then the world exploded.

CHAPTER EIGHTEEN

The first skunk ape burst out of the water inches from Mick, emitting a roar that was loud enough to deafen anyone near. Its hairy arms were extended outward as if to gather Mick and Dominic in a killing embrace. The little they could see of its face—exaggerated, human features that held nary a shred of humanity—was locked in a grimace of pure malevolence.

Liz brought her gun down to take a shot, but the guys were in the way.

The skunk ape took a swipe at Mick, catching him across the chest, sending him spinning. An arc of blood cascaded from his chest. She saw three horrific slashes open up from his neck down to his ribcage.

"Mick!" Dominic screamed.

He didn't give the skunk ape time to turn its attention on him, instead lunging at it with the sharp rock and smashing it into the side of its skull. The skunk ape shrieked and staggered backward.

"Dominic, get out of the way!" Rooster shouted.

Liz, Maddie and Jack were at the ready. They just needed a clear shot.

Dominic continued his assault, bringing the rock down in frenzied jabs on the skunk ape's head and shoulders. "You piece of shit! You wanna fuck with me? Come on, motherfucker!"

Mick had recovered and, though bleeding heavily, fired his gun. He missed badly, and Liz saw the grimace of pain on his face. The recoil must have brought waves of fire to his shredded chest.

Rooster churned up the murky water in a dash to help Dominic. The kid and the skunk ape had locked into one writhing mass.

Liz nudged Maddie. "Come on. If we get closer, we can take a shot."

Jack trailed behind them, his hand shaking like he was standing stark naked at the tip of the North Pole.

Dominic continued to whale on the skunk ape, loosing a string of epithets that were close to historic in their abandon. Rooster charged with the machete high above his head, ready to cleave the skunk ape in two.

The second skunk ape must have been lying in wait. It came up and planted a shoulder in Rooster's chest like he was a tackle dummy in football practice. Rooster was airborne, landing on his back with a tremendous splash a good ten feet from where the skunk ape hit him.

"Now!" Liz screamed, and she and Maddie each fired on it. It dove back into the water with reflexes impossible to comprehend.

"Did you hit it?" Jack shouted.

Liz didn't have time to answer. Dominic was still in hand-to-hand combat, and winning. She had to help him!

Mick floated on his back, unconscious. Maddie had gone to help Rooster, who was up and holding his chest.

Hell had ascended from the swamp's depths.

"Die, you piece of shit!" Dominic screamed. The rock had fallen out of his hand, and he repeatedly punched the skunk ape between the eyes. Its face was a red, pulpy mess.

The other skunk ape reappeared and grabbed Dominic's wrist before he could land another blow. Liz heard the crack of Jack's gun and felt the bullet whiz past her shoulder. It winged the skunk ape high in the shoulder. It wasn't enough to stop it from pulling Dominic's arm all the way back until it cracked. Dominic howled in agony. The skunk ape gave another quick tug, and Dominic's arm pulled free from his body.

Liz fired, cursing when she saw the bullet kick up water inches from the beast.

Blood pumped out of Dominic's side like a garden hose set to high. The one that he had been beating saw its chance at retribution and lunged forward, taking a bite out of his neck.

The skunk apes dove under the water, this time with Dominic.

Everyone watched in horror as the water rippled with the skunk apes' escape, heading to the west with the speed of a dolphin. Dominic's blood rested on the surface like an oil slick.

Rooster shouted, "Fuuuuuck!"

Liz heard Mick groan, and she rushed to his side. She almost gagged when she saw his exposed rib cage.

"Did you get it?" he wheezed.

Her eyes burned from tears. "Just…just stay still. I'll pull you onto the shore."

Rooster, Maddie and Jack were now beside them. Maddie was sobbing and Rooster's eyes were glazed over.

Jack helped Liz keep Mick propped up, and they headed for the island.

No one was prepared for the third skunk ape when it catapulted out of the shallow water, heading straight for Maddie.

"Noooooooooooo!" Liz screamed.

The skunk ape, the female of the clan, dropped over Maddie like a one-ton net. The girl didn't even have time to react or scream. One second she was by Rooster's side; the next, both she and the creature were gone.

Jack started shooting at the water, until Liz hammered his arm down.

"Stop it! You might hit my sister!" Tears streaked down her face.

Rooster felt numb. The throbbing pain in his chest faded. All that mattered was finding Maddie.

The water was placid. Not even a bubble to give him a direction to go in. The machete was weightless in his hand. All of the blood in his body felt like it was pooling in his arm, delivering the strength he'd need to hack the fucking ape into a million pieces.

"Maddie! Maddie!" Liz wailed. She trudged in circles through the water, desperately looking for a sign that her sister was nearby.

Jack held on to Mick, who was bleeding out fast and mumbling incoherently.

Liz and Rooster shouted for Maddie, but their cries were met with silence.

It wasn't until ten minutes had passed that he put an arm around Liz and said, "She's gone."

Liz smacked his hand away. "Don't fucking touch me! She's not gone! She's not!"

"Jack, can you get Mick to land?"

Jack nodded, pulling Mick along by his shoulders.

Rooster stayed close to Liz, letting her cry, giving her all the time she needed before hope ran out. It was quite a while before she stopped, closed her eyes and crashed into his chest, sobbing. He picked her up and carried her the rest of the way, laying her gently down among fallen palm leaves.

"Rooster."

Mick had gone deathly pale. Blood seeped out of his chest and formed a pool around his sides.

"Yeah," Rooster said, the effort of talking almost too much to bear.

"We at your place? I hope that radio works. Call the goddamn army, have them smoke those hairy assholes out." He laughed, and thick, dark mucous spluttered from his lips.

Rooster put a hand on Mick's leg. "We made it. I'll personally make sure the army gets every last one of them."

Mick closed his eyes. "Good. I think I might need a doctor." His breath came out in hitching gasps. "Might take a nap until he gets here, though. I'm beat."

He squeezed his leg. "You do that, brother. You earned it."

Mick's chest heaved once, and deflated slowly, the air gurgling in his throat.

Jack pushed two fingers against Mick's neck. "He's gone."

Rooster buried his head in his hands. Liz whimpered beside him.

It *took Maddie! I was right there, and it took her without a struggle.*

He pictured Dominic getting the better part of that fucker, replayed his arm being torn off. He looked at Mick's savaged corpse, at Liz's defeated gaze, at Jack's paralyzing fear.

Something in Rooster snapped.

He wasn't tired, or scared, or hurt.

He was mad.

So fucking mad, he wanted to tear the world in half.

And he knew just where to start.

PART THREE
FIGHT

CHAPTER NINETEEN

Rooster lifted Liz to her feet. She had gone so slack, it felt as if her bones had turned to putty. He knew it had to be devastating to lose a sister, but a twin? Well, that had to be almost too much to bear. It must have been like losing half of yourself. She was crying so much, she had started to hyperventilate.

"Get over here, Jack," he said. The little man had been staring at Mick's ravaged body, transfixed. He snapped to with a shake of his head and held Liz's arm.

The dark clouds were rolling in, seeping into the corners of Rooster's mind. Just like at Cheech's apartment, he was going to let them come, unhindered. He needed this to be the motherfucker of all storms, something that would quake and slash with ceaseless abandon. It had to last long enough for him to put an end to the fucking madness.

It had been two days since he'd taken his meds, and the dull buzz they cocooned him within was gone, leaving him free to feel and hate and act.

The first thing he had to do was get Liz back. She and her sister were the toughest chicks he'd ever come across, from clocking him out on the boat, to knowing how to shoot and survive, to not complaining for a single moment as they fled the murderous Bigfoots. He needed her strength and resolve. Which meant he had to force her into the storm.

He placed his hands on either side of her face and drew her gaze to his own. Her pupils were dilated, and she had the look of someone who had seen the end of the world and lived to suffer with the images.

"Liz, I need you to come back to me," he said softly, yet sternly. "If you want those bastards to pay for what they did to Maddie, I'm going to need you with me. Take a deep breath. That's it. Okay, now another, but try to hold it in for a bit. There. Keep doing that until you feel yourself settle."

Clarity seeped across her face like a slow-moving lava flow. It took several minutes, but the crying stopped, and all that was left was to wipe away the tears.

He looked over at Jack, expecting to see a rabbit preparing to run. To his surprise, Jack looked ready for anything.

"How far do you think your safe house is?" Jack asked.

Rooster scratched the coarse stubble on his chin. "Could be a couple of miles, if we're heading the right way. But we're not going there."

Jack stepped back, looking like Rooster had slapped him.

"What do you mean we're not going there? That's where the radio is so we can call for help! And why aren't there any search parties? I keep waiting to hear helicopters or at least a damn boat! It's like we fell into a *Twilight Zone* episode. I keep thinking, did we die when the boat wrecked? Is this hell?"

That gave Rooster pause. True, it felt like they were in the fiery depths, and you could definitely consider those monsters demons. He wasn't a religious man, but Jack's words gave him a moment of doubt.

"Do you know how big the Glades are? You might never hear that copter or boat. There are over ten thousand islands out here. This place is as remote and desolate as it was during the days of Columbus. And we are far off the tourist-beaten path. Out here, most times, the missing stay missing.

"We're not going to the cabin until we finish this shit. I'm tired of running; tired of being picked off like clay pigeons. You're going to fucking do what I fucking say, and when I say we're ready, then we can head to the cabin. You hear me?"

Rooster's chest heaved and he could feel the anger boiling over. He didn't even notice when Liz grabbed his arm. "I'll do whatever you say," she said, her breath still hitching in her chest.

He looked at Jack with his coldest, deadest stare. It was a look that had broken men a hundred times tougher than him. Jack averted his gaze as best he could, looking down and mumbling, "Okay, I'm in."

"Good. Let's get into the trees more. I have an idea."

"What about Mick?" Jack asked.

Rooster looked down at the pilot, wishing he was the one still on his feet. This was no time for pussies.

"Nothing we can do," he said. "Circle of life." He grabbed Jack by the collar. "Come on!"

The trees here were close together, with thick trunks and heavy leaves that blocked out the sun. As they walked, Rooster pulled out the last of their supplies and gave them out. "Might as well eat and drink what's left now. You're going to need your strength. We'll worry about later if there is a later."

He downed the bottle of soda and tore the cellophane off a cereal bar. The bar was gone in one bite.

Pointing down at the plastic case that Liz had somehow managed to cling to, he asked her to pop it open. Inside lay the waterlogged flare gun and three useless flares.

"Well, so much for that." He sighed. They couldn't catch a single break, and it was pissing him off mightily. For a moment, he had dared to dream of setting a flare off in one of their halitosis pie holes. He tossed the case over his shoulder.

Seeing that also made him become aware that he had left the money bag back in the water. He looked over the now-still surface and saw nothing. *Double fuck!* Now even if he did get out, he had zip to disappear with. Cortez would be on him like fat asses at a barbecue.

But this wasn't just about him.

Every inch of Liz and Jack's exposed skin was pocked with red bumps and welts from countless mosquito bites and scratches from bushes and tree branches. Seeing Liz like that was like seeing Maddie, which added to the intensity of his personal hurricane. They walked for ten minutes while he scanned the treetops. When he found what he was looking for, he said, "This will do."

"Do you see something?" Liz asked. She had fully regained her composure, what he assumed was a temporary state so she could get to the business at hand. There would be plenty of time for grieving. At least he hoped there would be.

He pointed upward. "I sure do. See the way those limbs converge? That's a perfect blind. You and I are going up there. Jack, you're staying down here. I want you to lie on the ground and start hollering like you're really hurt."

"I *am* hurt," Jack said.

"I mean hurt all to shit! I need you to sound desperate, weak, vulnerable."

Jack shook his head. "I see where this is going. You want me to be bait!"

"You must have been the smartest kid in your class," Rooster said with unrestrained sarcasm.

"No way. I'm not going to sit around waiting for one of those skunk apes to tear me apart while you play Tarzan with Jane over there. That's suicide."

Rooster's jaw clenched so hard it felt like his molars would explode. He was about to tell Jack that he would be the one to hurt him when Liz jumped between them.

"Wait! I'll do it as long as Jack gives me his gun. I want a backup in case things don't turn out the way we planned."

She held out her hand. Relieved, Jack was only too eager to hand his gun over.

Rooster laid a hand on her shoulder. "You sure about this? I can *make* him do it." He shot a glance at Jack, who looked like he had just wet himself.

"I'm not afraid. Not anymore."

She tucked the gun into the front of her jeans so it was nestled against her stomach.

"I'll be right up there. When the time comes, you and me are gonna make them wish they never fucked with us." He pointed at Jack. "Asshole, start climbing."

Jack scampered up the tree with a good deal of difficulty. Liz lay down at the base of the tree and moaned. Rooster made the climb with the ease of King Kong going up the Empire State

Building. The tree limbs were sturdy enough to support both their weights.

"Let it rip," he called down to Liz.

She began to wail in agony, calling out for them to come back for her. He had to give it to her. She sounded like her leg had been snapped in two. Her cries were piercing. In between her labored screams were tears. He knew they were tears for Maddie, just as her false shouts of pain were for Maddie's revenge.

It didn't take long for it to work. The Bigfoots' rotten stench wafted over them.

He tightened his grip on the machete, and waited.

CHAPTER TWENTY

Liz's scream caught in her throat the moment the skunk ape's nauseating smell wormed its way into her nose. Instead, she gagged, fighting the desperate need to vomit. She couldn't afford to lose whatever scant fluids she had left in her body, and she sure as hell didn't want to be wracked with spasms when death was so close. Her heart went crazy, like a wild horse set free. She prayed Rooster knew what he was doing. She'd seen the murderous look in his eye, and knew in that instant that he was no stranger to death.

Thinking about Maddie got her to calm down, to focus. Yes, they had killed the skunk ape child, but it had been an accident. In return, the creatures had taken six lives in the most brutal fashion conceivable.

In the small amount of time they had been together, it was easy for her to see that Rooster had feelings for Maddie. She'd always been the charmer. And despite what he was, her sister seemed to be falling for him. Maybe it was all a case of Stockholm Syndrome, but it did unite Liz and Rooster in one thing: neither would stop until every last one of those skunk apes was dead. Both sides had adopted a policy of mutually assured destruction, and neither gave a shit anymore.

She looked around, still doing her best to whimper softly and sound like easy pickings.

A pair of red eyes poked out from behind a tree.

At most, the beast was ten feet away.

Huff.

Was it calling to the others? Or was that just a grunt of satisfaction, knowing it had her dead to rights?

"Please, if you can hear me, I'm hurt! Help me!" Liz hoped that would lure the beast closer. She cried, hot tears spattering the dirt.

Old leaves shuffled, and she looked up to see the hulking shadow separate from the tree trunk. It wasn't the big mother, but it was massive nonetheless. It stared at her, chest heaving, eyes locked on to her. She saw its lips curl back over razor-sharp teeth.

"No! No!"

She raised an arm across her head and inched the gun out of her waistband with the other, careful not to let it see that she was armed. -The skunk apes had been shot at several times now. Even dumb animals could learn, and these things were not dumb.

It took three quick strides, stopped and screeched as if it thought the simple act of bellowing at her could kill her.

It didn't hear Rooster leap from his hiding place, a war cry spitting from his throat. The machete connected with the skunk ape's back before Rooster's feet hit the ground, a tactic meant to utilize gravity, momentum and Rooster's full weight so he could bury the machete deep.

The skunk ape howled in pain, pulling away from Rooster. The machete was firmly lodged in its back. It twisted round and round like a dog chasing its tail, desperate to locate the source of its pain. As the handle spun his way, Rooster grabbed hold, put one foot on the skunk ape's hip, and pulled with both hands. The machete came loose with a tearing sound and a jet of blood that colored Rooster from head to toe.

"How do you like it, motherfucker?" Rooster wailed. The skunk ape fell to its knees, loosing a series of low, rapid grunts.

Rooster didn't give it a chance to regain its footing. He brought the machete down on its skull with an earsplitting *crack*. The tip of the blade poked out from between its eyes. He worked the machete up and down, up and down, trying to pull it free. The moment he did, with gray brain matter flicking off the edge, he began hacking at both sides of its neck. Arterial spray whooshed out with an audible hiss. Liz caught a mouthful and spat out the vile-tasting plasma.

"Teach…you…fuckers to…fuck…with Rooster!" He drove the machete down into every section of the creature's body, like a chef chopping an onion in rapid motion. In under a minute, the skunk ape was nothing more than a mass of red, stringy fur, exposed bone and severed organs pouring out of fresh-made crevices.

"Rooster!" Liz shouted.

He stopped, looking at her with dazed eyes.

"It's dead," she said. "Save your strength. We have more to go."

He looked down at his hands as if they had just been attached moments ago. Between the blood and the wild look in his eyes, Liz would have sworn he was the Devil himself. But that didn't scare her. She needed the Devil to kill the demonic things that had murdered her sister.

A loud splash gave them both a start, distracting them from the quivering bits of the skunk ape.

Jack was still in the tree, vomiting hard. "Oh, my God, the smell," he said between heaves.

If living skunk apes smelled bad, dead ones that had been flayed open were even worse.

When Jack stopped, he wiped his mouth with the back of his arm and said, "I'd always heard the smell of blood was awful, but I think you may have nicked whatever gland made it reek so bad. Maybe they're not just rotten on the outside."

"Might as well come down," Liz said. "It's not like we can do the same thing here twice."

Jack hit the ground and rolled into his own vomit.

He was about to protest when Rooster raised his finger to his lips.

"You hear that?" he asked.

Liz tried, but could only discern the natural sounds of small critter life on the island. Rooster hadn't even bothered to wipe a drop of the blood from his face. It dripped down his cheeks, seeping into his mouth.

He pointed to the east. "They're over there."

"I didn't hear anything," Jack said.

"Trust me. Your nose will know I'm right."

He turned and headed off without waiting to see if they would follow. Liz helped Jack to his feet.

"I'm sure the rest of them will all be together, so get ready to use that," she said, handing the gun back to him. Jack needed it more than her. He nodded, and they scrambled to catch up with

Rooster, who Liz now felt with all her soul had become more beast than man.

She could hear her daddy telling her, *Stay close to him. If you want to survive, you have to put yourself in the eye of the hurricane. Remember everything I taught you. Don't let me or your sister down.*

She stopped when she spotted a branch that was just wide enough for her to stretch her fingers around. It must have been snapped off in a storm. The tip had split into a jagged, sharp point. The guns hadn't done them much good. Time for a new tactic.

CHAPTER TWENTY-ONE

Damn, it felt good to make mincemeat out of that friggin' ape.

Rooster was riding his anger high, hard and fast. Back there, carving up that fucker like it was a Thanksgiving turkey that had done him wrong, he didn't even feel the blood as it bathed his skin or smell the hellish funk that oozed out of each chopped-up bit. It was like an out-of-body experience, this free rein given to his anger, letting it satisfy its every lust and hunger.

Maybe that's why all those folks back home tried their damndest to wring that poison out of me, he thought. As he ran recklessly, he briefly wondered what his life would be like after this—if there was an after. Would his anger all bleed out, or would it continue to boil? Then he thought of Maddie, and realized he didn't give a crap. He had work to do.

He skidded to a stop when he saw a pair of hairy, enormous skulls just above a line of bushes. They were facing the other way, oblivious to his approach. He jerked around and motioned for Jack and Liz to freeze.

"Two, up ahead," he mouthed.

Liz's mouth set in a grim line. Jack hunched low, looking nervous as all get out.

He waved them to come closer.

"Liz, I say we flank them while Jack here empties out that gun the moment they stand up. Looks like you found a spear. Nice. Just drive it into its belly, where you won't get much resistance. You try for the chest or head and it'll just bounce off the bone. Drive it deep as you can and just keep pushing on it."

"Got it."

"And Jack, I need you to be fucking Wild Bill Hickok. Make the few shots you have count. Go for their upper backs. With any luck, you'll hit their spine. That'll drop 'em quick. Just breathe through your mouth and keep your eyes open when you pull the trigger."

Jack was already doing his share of mouth breathing to calm his nerves. His head bobbed up and down like a bird dipping into a puddle of water.

"Just let me lead. Liz, once you see me, you comeready to gore its ugly ass. I'll take the right. Let's hit it before they go looking for their dead brother."

Liz gave him a thumbs-up and disappeared behind a cypress tree without making a sound. Rooster wasn't quite as nimble, but in a way, he wanted the Bigfoots to know he was coming. He hoped when he got close enough, they could smell the blood of their brother on him. He wanted them to feel what it was like to be hunted. Most of all, he wanted them to feel fear.

The trees ended in a flat field of high grass. He emerged from the tree line about fifteen feet to the right of the sitting Bigfoots. Both looked hurt, the worse being the one Dominic had done a number on. Its face was jacked to hell and looked like a mask made of crumbled bologna. The other was nursing its arm and grimacing in pain.

Perfect.

No sense waiting for someone to ring the bell.

Rooster charged, holding the machete across his chest with both hands like a samurai brandishing his sword. Their heads twitched to face him, and he noticed that the one Dominic had pummeled was missing both its eyes. *Even better, because that would be Liz's kill.*

The gunshot one rose up and did its best to let out one of those tighty-whitey-staining roars, but it didn't have the strength. Rooster saw Liz dart out from behind something that looked like a termite mound with her makeshift spear pointed in the beast's direction.The Bigfoot swiped at him with its long arm, but he ducked and slashed with the machete across its belly. He heard Jack's gun go off and saw the other one stagger when the bullet buried itself in its back. Rooster hadn't gotten near enough of the Bigfoot's belly, so he went to take a hack at its good shoulder. The damn thing still had some speed left in it, and it dodged the blow, catching him with a backhand that sent him ass over head.

He stopped tumbling just in time to see Liz go for bologna face's gut. She misjudged, aimed too high, and sure enough, the branch hit the bottom of its rib cage and shuddered out of her hands.

"Liz!"

Scrabbling to his feet, he watched in horror as the other Bigfoot sprinted toward Liz. He ran, shouting as loud as he could to get its attention.

When it turned, swinging both arms to tear his head from his neck, he dropped low like he was sliding into second base, letting the momentum carry him forward, where he slashed at its leg, rending a gaping maw in its calf. There was another shot, and he saw bologna face's head explode like an egg in a microwave. Jack let out a cry of exultation, and Liz jumped back to avoid having the big ape fall on her.

One to go.

The last Bigfoot backed away slowly, limping and trailing blood and stink that even Mother Nature couldn't wash away.

"That's right, big fella. It's me and you now," Rooster sneered. He advanced, swinging the machete in a wide arc. The Bigfoot put up a hand to stop it and lost three fingers for its efforts. It yelped and paused to look at its wrecked hand.

"I may just save those fingers for myself. Maybe they'll be lucky, like a rabbit's foot."

All the Bigfoot could do was cower, even though it stood a good foot and a half taller than him and outweighed him considerably. Its fear fed Rooster's rage, and he growled as he swept in to deliver the killing blow.

"Jack!"

Liz's scream caused just enough of a hitch in his swing for the Bigfoot to twist out of harm's way. The machete sliced into the grass with a resounding *thud.*

Rooster looked over and saw Liz pointing in the trees. When he looked back at the Bigfoot, it was gone!

"Rooster!" Liz shouted, waving frantically for him.

When he got to her side, he pulled up short and swallowed back bile.

The mother Bigfoot, all nine feet or so of her, had pinned Jack's arms to his sides and held him off the ground like you'd lift a plastic lawn chair. It grunted at them, and Rooster could feel the hate in its scarlet glare.

"Don't come any closer!" Jack warned. His voice came out in a pained rush.

"Rooster, we have to do something," Liz pleaded.

That's when he saw Jack's eyes travel downward, and knew the little guy had a plan up his sleeve.

CHAPTER TWENTY-TWO

Rooster turned to her and said, "Liz, I want you to look away."

"What?"

She had to have heard him wrong.

"I need you to get behind me and don't look at Jack until I tell you to."

"But—"

"Don't argue with me!"

His big hand rested on her hip and guided her behind him.

Her mind flew in a hundred different directions. She'd already seen people torn to pieces and watched her own sister disappear under the crushing weight of one of those animals. If she and Rooster attacked the mother skunk ape, maybe it would let Jack go and they could, at the very least, scare it off.

The tension in Rooster's voice and grip told her there was no room for argument. She slipped behind his broad back, felt the heaving of his chest. The sky darkened and the smell of rain infused the air. She twitched when Jack yelled, and had to bite the palm of her hand to keep from running to his aid.

"Aaagggh, it hurts!" Jack wailed. The mother Bigfoot didn't take its eyes off Rooster. It was using Jack as a warning or a threat—or, most likely, a promise. *This is what I have in store for you.* There was something almost human in its penetrating gaze. Only humans had the capacity to hate, to seek revenge, to kill for the sake of killing.

Rooster gave back as much as he took.

"You just hang in there," he said flatly.

When he'd first spied Jack, his impulse had been to charge and let the machete do all the talking. When he saw the gun in Jack's hand, he forced himself to hold back.

"I've got…at least…one bullet left," Jack wheezed.

The Bigfoot growled, low and menacing, and a thick line of drool fell from its mouth onto Jack's cheek.

"I think I…hear…more of them."

More of them? Rooster hoped he meant the one that got away and had retreated to the rear, sans one third of its fingers.

Rooster tensed when the Bigfoot opened its mouth wide, so wide it looked like it could swallow a cantaloupe whole, and slowly took in the top of Jack's head. Teeth that were as jagged as snapped timber punctured his scalp and scraped downward. Jack's eyes went wide and his body went rigid.

When Rooster took a half step forward, Jack shouted, "Don't!"

Jack's right arm was free enough so he could still bend at the elbow. He raised the gun up as high as he could, until it was pointing directly under his chin.

There was a sickening sound of crunching as the Bigfoot moved its lower jaw from side to side, gouging deep gullies into his skull. Blood flowed in racing rivulets down his face. The pain must have been excruciating.

"Jack, you don't have to do that!" Rooster yelled.

The urge to grind that mother up into chop meat was burning his soul to ashes.

"I'm...dead...anyway. Be nice...to take...charge for...once."

Rooster saw the Bigfoot flex its arms and apply more pressure to Jack's body. It leered at Rooster while it mouthed Jack's head like an ice pop. The fucking thing was getting off watching Rooster stand there, helpless.

You've got a surprise coming, asshole.

Blood bubbled from the creature's mouth, and for a second Jack looked like he was going to pass out. His eyes rolled back, and he shut his lids tight. His finger pulled on the trigger.

The blast was quick and true. The bullet entered just under his chin, sprouting a fountain of gore.

The Bigfoot jerked its head back so quickly, it brought the top of Jack's skull right off. Jack's brains cascaded several feet into the air. The bullet must have ricocheted off part of his skull, because it didn't travel straight through and into the Bigfoot's mouth. Instead, it came out the side of Jack's head and cut a deep furrow into the damned thing's left cheek. It dropped Jack's body and howled in surprise, pain and anger.

"Get ready," Rooster said to Liz. He was shit-sure it was going to charge them like a riled-up bull.

Instead, it balled its hands into tight firsts, bent at the waist and roared at him before charging back into the woods.

Shit! You're going the wrong way, Rooster lamented.

He spun around to face Liz. "I'm going to give you a choice and you have five seconds to decide. You can either come with me while I track down that son of a bitch, or you can hole up in one of the trees and wait for me. When I get back, I'll get us to my father's safe house."

Liz saw Jack's body on the ground and quickly replied, "Let's go."

Both Bigfoots ran recklessly, tearing down anything in their path. Following the sounds of their mad dash, and their overwhelming scent that only seemed to intensify, was easy. Rooster called up reserves of energy from every cell in his body to keep close behind. Liz was also holding her own.

The clouds finally burst, and rain came in driving buckets. In less time than it takes to change your underwear, the ground had transformed into a muddy mess. More than a couple of times, Rooster lost his footing and almost took a header.

They were close!

"Eeeeeaaaaaaaaaaagggggggghhhhhh!" he shouted at the top of his lungs. He wanted them to know he was on their tails, that death was just a moment away.

Suddenly, the heavy sounds of their escape ceased.

"What the hell?"

Liz ran into him. "Sound like they're tired of running. They must be hoping we run right into them, the way Maddie and I set them up last night."

Rooster swung the machete at a branch near his face, sending the branch spiraling to the soggy ground. "Well, I'd hate to disappoint them."

He plunged ahead, his voice raw from screaming like a wild man.

Something snatched his foot and he hit the ground on his side, sliding in the mud until his head cracked into a hardwood tree.

The Bigfoot without its fingers rose up from a stand of downed branches and leaves. Before Rooster could get back to his feet, it was on him, latching on to his leg and squeezing hard enough to make his thigh pop. Pain only stoked the fires of his fury.

He swooped the machete upward, burying it into the monster's arm. The Bigfoot flinched, and the machete, still in its arm, was pried loose from Rooster's hand.

Ignoring the blade, the Bigfoot dropped to all fours and scampered until it was directly over him. Hot drool spattered his face as it huffed and growled. It was the first time Rooster had been so close, their noses just inches from one another. There was nothing remotely human about it. The beast that pinned him to the mud was no missing link, no offshoot of the simian tree. It was something altogether different, culling the darker, more savage parts of both species.

Rooster tried to roll out from under its incredible girth, but it stopped him cold with a solid punch to the ground, burying its hairy fist into the muck.

Well, fuck me sideways. Never saw my end coming this way.

"Go ahead, kill me," Rooster hissed, recoiling from the rancid breath that blew over him in steady waves. "But always remember, I got your kid *and* your brothers, you big, stupid son of a bitch!"

CHAPTER TWENTY-THREE

The skunk ape's attention was fully on Rooster. Liz checked around for the bigger, meaner mother, but it was hard to see or hear anything in the downpour. She only had one chance and no time to hesitate.

Pushing all of her survival instincts aside, she ran hard, vaulting atop the creature's shoulders armed with nothing but her own two hands and her fading hopes at avenging Maddie's death.

She grabbed hold of the coarse hair that matted its neck and tugged with all of her might. It pulled back and tried to butt her with the back of its head, but she was quick and shifted sideways. Rooster was still locked beneath it. She pulled harder, driving her knees into its side, hoping there was a kidney nearby that would not take kindly to the pressure.

"Get…off of him!" she keened.

It shook from side to side like a dog shuddering water from its fur. She fought to keep her purchase. When it swung its arms back to snatch her, the handle of the machete struck her in the ribs and punched every bit of air from her lungs. The impact dislodged the machete from the skunk ape's arm and it clanged against a tree root. She gasped, loosening her fingers and flipping off the wounded creature's back. Liz hit the ground and spots danced before her eyes. Rainwater filled her open mouth as she fought for breath. She felt she would drown in the process.

Liz turned to her side to force the water to run out. It also meant she had turned her back on the skunk ape. She was close to blacking out. Her diaphragm hitched uncontrollably, and it felt like an eternity since she had last felt the cool kiss of oxygen.

An iron claw wrapped itself around her ankle, and she was suddenly upside down and staring at the ground. Everything sounded so far away. Nothing made sense. The neurons in her brain misfired, and a growing numbness shot through her extremities.

She was having a hard time keeping her eyes focused, though she did see Rooster rise up from the ground, his machete pointed outward down by his waist. He resembled every childhood nightmare of the bogeyman, except this one *murdered* the monster under your bed.

The machete sliced through the air, and suddenly she was level with the ground. She finally felt her body relax, and her mind went blank.

Rooster cackled as he watched the Bigfoot toss about, staring wide-eyed at the spot where its hand used to be. Blood came out in long, stuttering streams.

He hammered the machete into its shoulder, cleaving the base of its neck. That stopped its bawling. He ran behind it, slicing where its Achilles tendons should be. It dropped to its knees, bleeding out, unable to walk. Next, he took off its other hand.

It whimpered on the ground, trembling from shock.

Rooster felt no pity.

He straddled its chest, made sure to look it dead in the eye, and pushed the tip of the machete deep, right below the arch of the breastbone.

He watched it die, waited until its eyes clouded over. It wasn't the first time he'd seen death pluck the soul from a body. When he was sure the deed was done, he spit into its gaping mouth, plucking the machete out with a loud *squish*.

Only momma left.

Liz was still out cold, but her chest was rising steadily.

He couldn't bring her with him to get the mother. It was too big, too dangerous. And like him, it had cold hatred in its heart.

Looking around, he found the makeshift hideout that the Bigfoot had built to ambush him. Carrying Liz away from the body, he repositioned the branches so they camouflaged her. Wiping her hair from her face, he knelt down and whispered, "I don't know if you can hear me, but I need you to sit tight. I'm going after the last one, but I'm coming back for you. My daddy's place isn't far now. I don't know how I know that, but it just feels right. Jesus, I hope you don't get up and wander, because there's no telling how lost you'll get out here. Just sleep for now. I ain't leaving this swamp without you."

There was no way of knowing if she comprehended a single word, but he had to try.

The rain was relentless, and dark shadows nestled into every corner of the woods.

It was obvious the mother was nowhere nearby, or else she was a ruthless bitch, watching one of her kin get carved to pieces. Rooster would have to be smarter if he wanted a chance to get at her. He'd never been much of a hunter, of animals at least, but there'd been enough hunting trips when he was a kid to draw upon.

He looked at the steaming remains of the Bigfoot. His nose was oblivious to the stench now.

That was it!

The only way to sneak up on the momma was to somehow make her believe he was one of her family. "Oh, Jesus H. Christmas, this is not gonna be fun."

Using the edge of his machete, he sawed away at the Bigfoot's hide, pulling the fur and upper layers of its flesh from the bone. His skinning work was rough, bordering on brutal, but it didn't need to be pretty. When he was done, he had pulled off enough to drape over his head and shoulders, with long, blood-soaked strips swaying at his knees.

To combat the rain from washing the scent off of him, he reached into its exposed entrails and pulled out what he could, rubbing it across his chest, legs and arms. He grabbed a rope of intestine, leaving some to trail out of his pockets, and stuffed something that looked like a liver into his shirt.

He threw up when he felt the quivering organ against his bare stomach, and again when the meaty skull cap dipped low and over his nose and mouth.

"There," he spat, his hands on his knees. "Nothing left to toss now."

A cluster of thunderclaps sounded off in the distance. He straightened up, took a deep breath and headed into the deepest part of the woods.

CHAPTER TWENTY-FOUR

If he was right, this particular island ended in another eighth of a mile. The opposite end should be a big sandbar. He walked as heavily as he could to mimic the Bigfoot's thunderous gait. The one drawback to wearing the flesh and organs of the Bigfoot was that he couldn't use his nose to sniff out the momma. It had overwhelmed his senses so much, he was probably immune to it.

But if he was lucky, the sand would tell him all he needed to know.

It took a while to get there because he didn't go in a straight line. He zigzagged and backtracked so he could give momma ample evidence that she was not alone. She didn't come out to greet or maim him. She was either hiding low, waiting to trap him like the other one, or she had moved on. He pushed any thoughts of the bitch-beast going back for Liz.

No, Liz would be there when he got back.

If he got back.

He came to the beach and nearly genuflected with joy.

A pair of tracks, the biggest goddamn feet he'd ever seen, led from the tree line right to the water's edge. Another island beckoned to him, a mere fifty or so yards away. There was sand there, too. Rooster plodded into the water, heedless of the other wildlife that could kill him just as easily as the Bigfoot. He didn't know if God or the Devil were looking after him know, but he did know that neither would let it end with a bite by some damn snake. He draped the dripping skin over his arms, doing his best to keep them out of the water.

Sure enough, the footprints resumed on the next island. The rain had eased back a bit, so the prints were preserved pretty well. It couldn't have passed by here more than ten minutes earlier.

He stalked into the trees. Why did every island in this part have to have so many trees? There were too many places for momma to hide. He could be out here for the next ten years tracking the thing at this rate.

Somehow, he had to make it come to him.

The huffing noises they made! There were a couple of times he'd seen them do that, and it had looked like they were talking to each other. He wasn't a friggin' ventriloquist, but he thought he could imitate the sound. It was that or nothing.

Rooster settled against a palm tree, sliding onto his haunches. He tucked the blade within the wet strips of the Bigfoot hide.

He took several gulps of air, relaxed his throat.

The short grunts and pants sounded, to his ears, on the money. He imagined what a hurt Bigfoot would sound like, and tried to convey that emotion into his call. After several minutes, he stopped. The rain had moved off, but pregnant patters of drops still fell from the trees. He strained to listen.

Nothing.

So he started up again, pausing, starting, pausing, starting. He figured he'd give it a good half hour or more. If this didn't work, it was back to tracking through impossible terrain.

Gagging slightly, he extracted the liver from his shirt and pierced it with the machete. A new malodorous gust expelled from the split organ. He restarted his call in earnest, louder and louder, feeling the distress bleed from his pores.

Snap!

Whatever it was, it sounded large and deliberate, like a rotted log being stepped on. He kept up with his Bigfoot cry, keeping his eyes peeled.

The momma's crimson eyes peered out from behind a wide mahogany tree. He could sense its reluctance. No matter how good a job he thought he was doing, he was sure it sounded slightly off to the monster.

Better to stop, let the smell and disguise reel it the rest of the way in.

He tightened his hold on the machete. The Bigfoot came out from behind the tree and sniffed the air. Rooster moved his foot to catch its attention. Momma narrowed her eyes at him.

Come on, you big ugly bitch.

She startled him when she raced forward, stopping a couple of feet from him. It was amazing. One second she was a good fifteen yards away, and the next she was in his face. How could something so fucking big move so fast?

He'd kept his head down, until now.

His chin rose up, and the meaty skull cap slipped from the back of his head. The momma's eyes scrunched into tight, malevolent slits and her lips pulled back from teeth that could tear through an alligator's hide.

Rooster swung the blade, barely managing to nick its right shin. The Bigfoot jumped back and cried out in an uncontrolled rage. Both hands pawed the air, flexing open and closed, itching to get a piece of him.

Fat chance!

Rooster tugged the rest of the fur from his shoulder and flung it at the momma's face. It tried to dodge it, but the fur and skin wrapped around its head nonetheless. Not wasting a second, he cleaved its chest in one stroke, catching it on the inside of the elbow on the upswing.

It ripped its kin's hide from its face and lashed out, catching Rooster in the shoulder with fingers that were chiseled into talons. Three rivers of heat opened up on his flesh.

He countered with a swipe that severed the tip of its wide nose right off.

"Oh shit."

That particular blow sent it into an apoplectic rampage. It lashed out with a speed and intensity that no man could defend. He was kicked in the thigh, bashed on the chest and hammered on his wounded shoulder. The machete flew from his hands into the underbrush. The pain was unreal. Still the Bigfoot carried on with its frenzy. He was powerless to stop it, unable to ward off a single blow.

When it kicked him in the stomach, he felt his internal organs shift into places they weren't meant to be. He crashed onto the ground like a boxer who had taken a hard one to the chin. His arms flopped uselessly at his sides.

Momma stopped her convulsing when she realized he was down and done. She stood above him, chest heaving, urine flowing onto the ground and his legs.

He was marked. He was hers.

CHAPTER TWENTY-FIVE

The Bigfoot reached down and scooped him into her arms. Its pendulous breasts crushed his already shattered chest.

She wasn't about to play around with him. He had killed her child, and in turn she had killed everyone around him, losing the rest of her family in the process. Every ounce of venom running in her veins was directed at Rooster.

All he wanted now was to die. To make the pain stop.

Maybe this *was* hell. He hadn't deserved much else. If this was, the moment she killed him, it would start all over again.

He wondered how it would end for Liz.

Liz!

Dammit, he promised her he'd be back. But he had nothing left. Nada. Zip.

The Bigfoot's voice rumbled and it licked blood from its lips.

There was only one shot left to him. Rooster opened his mouth, and to his astonishment, the Bigfoot mimicked him. They stared at one another, slack-jawed, both seeming to wait the other out to see what the next move would be.

Rooster pushed his head forward and clamped down as hard as he could on the remains of its nose.

The Bigfoot screamed for the heavens to hear. She swatted his face, which freed an arm. He reached up and drove his thumb as deep into its eye as he could, stopping when he felt hot, membranous resistance.

She dropped onto her back. He did the same with his other hand, blinding it, probing for its brain to perform an Everglade lobotomy. Something popped under his thumbs, and the Bigfoot suddenly ceased moving, its final cry dying in its throat. His thumb slid easily into the hot, soft mass of its brain.

He rolled off her body and winced when his ribs struck the ground.

"Gotta make sure," he wheezed.

It took a few minutes to find the machete. His legs felt like cotton candy.

No sense fooling around. He slashed at its neck again and again until the head rolled free. The monster's body jerked with every blow, nerve endings caught in a death twitch.

Rooster staggered back to admire his kill. No one would ever believe this. In a couple of days, all of the Bigfoot bodies would be 'reclaimed' by the Everglades. Probably wouldn't even be bones left to have as a souvenir.

Fuck it. The rage high they'd given him was reward enough. Now maybe he could live a peaceful life.

Peace.

Rooster's world spun like a tilt-a-whirl, and he passed out.

"Rooster? Rooster?"

Liz cradled his head in her lap and poured small drops of rainwater she had collected in a palm leaf onto his mouth. The guy looked like he'd been through a meat grinder. She couldn't tell where his blood ended and the skunk ape's blood began. And beneath the blood were bruises so purple and black, she worried about internal bleeding.

She'd panicked when she'd woken up under the shelter, and in her daze set out searching for him without thinking the skunk ape could be near. When she saw the remains of their footprints at the shore, she came to this island and heard their struggle. It was like listening to two bears go at it whole hog, except one of the bears could talk and curse with the proficiency of a maestro.

By the time she found him, the skunk ape's head sat several feet from its body and Rooster lay on the ground. The whole scene looked as if it had been a fight to the death, until she saw his chest rise and fall. Then she set about doing what she could to take care of him. Without a full medical team nearby, there was little she could do other than wash some of the lacerations and stay by his side.

It had been four hours and he hadn't stirred. Night was coming fast. She had to wake him.

Liz tilted the palm leaf so the rest of the water splashed across his face. He winced, and a hand lazily tried to swipe the water off.

When his eyes did open, she smoothed his hair back and stroked his cheek.

"Am I dead?" he asked, his throat parched, hoarse.

"Not yet," Liz said and smiled. "Although I can't say the same for our skunk ape pal. I don't know how you did it."

He held his palm against the side of his head as he sat up. "A little something I learned from Rage Against the Machine. *Anger is a gift.*"

She gave him some time to get to his feet and set his bearings. The machete rested against her thigh, blood crusted over every square inch.

Rooster looked up. "I think we can make it to the shack before night."

Liz had never heard more magical words.

He pointed to the west. "It should be on the next island over. You think canned fruit can last nine years?"

She felt her stomach growl. "I'm willing to face the consequences if it can't. Here, rest on me." She pulled his arm across her shoulders. He laughed.

"After all this, you want to get crushed to death?"

"You should know by now, I'm tougher than I look."

Rooster nodded, and she felt more of his weight lean in to her.

Together, they limped away from the skunk ape's decapitated body, and the smell grew fainter with each step.

A lone gator watched them make the water crossing. Rooster asked Liz for the machete, but thankfully didn't need to use it. The reptilian eyes bobbed atop the water, following every painful step. At one point, the water washed over their heads and they had to swim. Every stroke brought fire to his arms and lungs. He breathed a sigh of relief when they made land.

A pink and purple dusk bathed the swamp, and he knew they had to double-time it.

"It's not far now, just a couple hundred yards," he said, spying a gumbo tree that his father had carved a series of deep notches and swirls into as a marker. Time had almost erased his handiwork. For the first time since jumping on the airboat, Rooster felt like he had some control.

"Does it have a bed?" Liz asked, still doing her best to prop him up.

"A couple of old army cots that probably have more mildew than a politician has bullshit."

She patted his back lightly. "That sounds like a night at the Ritz right about now."

There were a couple of times his head spun and he thought he was going to pass out, but Liz sensed the slackening in his body and swelled under him to keep him upright and moving. The chick was the goods, all right.

She let out a whoop when his father's cabin came into view. One side of the roof was sagging something fierce, and the local flora had grown so high around it that it looked like the earth was trying absorb it, board by board.

Thank you, Daddy. Sometimes, having a criminal father had its advantages.

Rooster straightened as if he'd been hit with a cattle prod.

That smell!

Liz had caught it, too, because she whispered, "Oh, no, there's more."

CHAPTER TWENTY-SIX

Rooster told Liz to stay and moved up closer to the cabin. She could hear a muffled commotion and her heart sank into her shoes.

The skunk apes were in the cabin.

She held her breath as Rooster, calling up a fifth or tenth wind, crept outside the cabin, peering inside the half-open door. She saw him clench his fists, and when he turned back, a dark veil of rage had descended over his face.

He walked to her and said, "I'm going to need the machete." His voice was atonal, like a zombie.

"You're in no condition to go in there. Maybe we can just wait them out, go in when they leave and see if there's anything salvageable."

"The machete." He held his meaty hand out, his arm steady as a steel girder.

"But–"

"Just give me the blade."

She reluctantly handed it to him. He stalked back toward the cabin. He wasn't sneaking this time. He wanted his presence to be known. She watched him stride through the door, and then the gates of hell opened up.

When Rooster looked inside the cabin, he had expected to find one or two of the Bigfoots. It made sense to use the place as a shelter. His first inclination was to hide out until they went out looking for the rest of their family or tribe or whatever the fuck they were.

Instead, what he witnessed was something that could not be tolerated, could not be waited out while cowering like a scared boy.

Maddie lay on the big oak table that he had helped his father cart out one nice early spring day.

Her skin was a dark blue. She was dead. At least there was closure on that front.

Around her stood five of the creatures, only smaller than the band that had been picking them off for the past two days. The tallest was maybe a little over five feet.

Bigfoot adolescents.

One was taking a turn at Maddie, its grotesque body between her legs and pumping like mad while the others hooted around it. They pawed her face and breasts while stroking what could only be their erections under their fur.

The rage he felt was unmatched by every angry moment he had ever experienced, combined. No one deserved this.

Maddie, above all, didn't deserve this.

They would pay, now, and with as much pain and suffering as he could administer.

Rooster knocked on the door with the end of the machete. The gawking Bigfoots stopped, but the one screwing her corpse continued with complete disregard.

"Well, now I know which one gets it first," he grumbled.

With the back of his foot, he kicked the door shut. These Bigfoots were nothing like the other ones. There was cold fear in their eyes. Most of them were scrawny, almost fragile. He was anxious to see just how fragile.

The others backed away when he swung the machete, catching the one with Maddie along the top of its head. A quarter-moon slice of its skull slipped away, and its brain bulged out of the opening. Still it pumped away.

Rooster felt the storm of his anger overtake him.

And it felt good.

When he emerged, he did his best to brush the bits of fur, skin and bone from his clothes, but it was impossible to get everything. Liz saw him and she made to run over.

"Stay there!" he shouted. "I'll bring out anything we can use."

Jesus, he could never let her see this. After massacring the Bigfoots, he had covered Maddie with an old wool blanket.

There were a couple of cans of peaches and pears, a tin of chewing tobacco, one cot that hadn't been bashed into splinters and not much else. The ham radio was in pieces. It looked like it had been smashed years ago. So much for calling for help.

He brought the cot and cans to Liz.

She twitched back slightly as she took hold of the cot, studying him like you would an agitated cobra. Shit, he didn't want to scare her, but he wasn't sure he would ever recover from this.

"Is...is the radio still there?"

He shook his head. "Here, lie down a bit. We're not going anywhere soon."

When he went back to the cabin, which now resembled the inside of a slaughterhouse run by wolverines, he pulled up one of the floorboards to see if there was anything in the secret stash. He found an old hurricane lamp, two lighters and a .38.

Guns. That's what had gotten him—hell, all of them—into this mess.

He took the hurricane lamp and smashed the top against the skull of one of the creatures. With a few flicks of his wrist, he doused the entire cabin with the kerosene.

After raising the blanket and looking at Maddie one last time, he flicked the lighter's wheel and tossed it on the larger pile of Bigfoot pieces to the rear of the small cabin. They caught with a tremendous *whoosh.*

Black tendrils of smoke followed him as he walked outside.

Liz stood by the cot, holding the cans to her chest.

Red and orange flames danced out of the lone window and licked the sides of the cabin.

"Maybe someone will see that," he said, and sat heavily onto the ground.

"Do you think there's a chance?" Liz said, her voice trancelike.

He considered it. "Well, we've been gone a couple of days, so the search would still be on. It's getting dark. Fire like that'll show up real nice."

They watched in silence as the fire consumed the cabin, the wood popping and spitting, setting a nearby tree alight.

He heard Liz sit on the cot and felt her hand on his shoulder.

"I wonder if there are more of them out here?" Liz said. "They could be watching us right now, or they could be on another island miles away. What are the chances we got them all?"

"I don't know, Liz. And as long as they stay the hell away from me, I don't fucking care."

The fire burned, night fell, and they waited.

CHECK OUT OTHER GREAT HORROR NOVELS

BLACK FRIDAY
by Michael Hodges

Jared the kleptomaniac, Chike the unemployed IT guy, Patricia the shopaholic, and Jeff the meth dealer are trapped inside a Chicago supermall on Black Friday. Bridgefield Mall empties during a fire alarm, and most of the shoppers drive off into a strange mist surrounding the mall parking lot. They never return. Chike and his group try calling friends and family, but their smart phones won't work, not even Twitter. As the mist creeps closer, the mall lights flicker and surge. Bulbs shatter and spray glass into the air. Unsettling noises are heard from within the mist, as the meth dealer becomes unhinged and hunts the group within the mall. Cornered by the mist, and hunted from within, Chike and the survivors must fight for their lives while solving the mystery of what happened to Bridgefield Mall. Sometimes, a good sale just isn't worth it.

GRIMWEAVE
by Tim Curran

In the deepest, darkest jungles of Indochina, an ancient evil is waiting in a forgotten, primeval valley. It is patient, monstrous, and bloodthirsty. Perfectly adapted to its hot, steaming environment, it strikes silent and stealthy, it chosen prey: human. Now Michael Spiers, a Marine sniper, the only survivor of a previous encounter with the beast, is going after it again. Against his better judgement, he is made part of a Marine Force Recon team that will hunt it down and destroy it.

The hunters are about to become the hunted.

CHECK OUT OTHER GREAT
HORROR NOVELS

DEATH CRAWLERS
by Gerry Griffiths

Worldwide, there are thought to be 8,000 species of centipede, of which, only 3,000 have been scientifically recorded. The venom of Scolopendra gigantea—the largest of the arthropod genus found in the Amazon rainforest—is so potent that it is fatal to small animals and toxic to humans. But when a cargo plane departs the Amazon region and crashes inside a national park in the United States, much larger and deadlier creatures escape the wreckage to roam wild, reproducing at an astounding rate. Entomologist, Frank Travis solicits small town sheriff Wanda Rafferty's help and together they investigate the crash site. But as a rash of gruesome deaths befalls the townsfolk of Prospect, Frank and Wanda will soon discover how vicious and cunning these new breed of predators can be. Meanwhile, Jake and Nora Carver, and another backpacking couple, are venturing up into the mountainous terrain of the park. If only they knew their fun-filled weekend is about to become a living nightmare

THE PULLER
by Michael Hodges

Matt Kearns has two choices: fight or hide. The creature in the orchard took the rest. Three days ago, he arrived at his favorite place in the world, a remote shack in Michigan's Upper Peninsula. The plan was to mourn his father's death and figure out his life. Now he's fighting for it. An invisible creature has him trapped. Every time Matt tries to flee, he's dragged backwards by an unseen force. Alone and with no hope of rescue, Matt must escape the Puller's reach. But how do you free yourself from something you cannot see?

CHECK OUT OTHER GREAT
HORROR NOVELS

MONSTROSITY
by Tim Curran

The Food. It seeped from the ground, a living, gushing, teratogenic nightmare. It contaminated anything that ate it, causing nature to run wild with horrible mutations, creating massive monstrosities that roam the land destroying towns and cities, feeding on livestock and human beings and one another. Now Frank Bowman, an ordinary farmer with no military skills, must get his children to safety. And that will mean a trip through the contaminated zone of monsters, madmen, and The Food itself. Only a fool would attempt it. Or a man with a mission

THE SQUIRMING
by Jack Hamlyn

You are their hosts

You are their food.

The parasites came out of nowhere, squirming horrors that enslaved the human race. They turned the population into mindless pack animals, psychotic cannibalistic hordes whose only purpose was to feed them.

Now with the human race teetering at the edge of extinction, extermination teams are fighting back, killing off the parasites and their voracious hosts. Taking them out one by one in violent, bloody encounters.

The future of mankind is at stake.

And time is running out.

Printed in Great Britain
by Amazon

63018436R00090